# Divine Son
# of Ra

# Divine Son of Ra

## JOANNA MAKEPEACE

G.K. Hall & Co. • Chivers Press

Thorndike, Maine USA     Bath, England

This Large Print edition is published by G.K. Hall & Co., USA and by Chivers Press, England.

Published in 1997 in the U.S. by arrangement with Margaret York.

Published in 1997 in the U.K. by arrangement with the author.

U.S.  Softcover   0-7838-2016-X   (Paperback Collection Edition)
U.K.  Hardcover   0-7451-8891-5   (Chivers Large Print)

The text of this Large Print edition is unabridged.
Other aspects of the book may vary from the original edition.

Set in 16 pt. News Plantin by Juanita Macdonald.

Printed in the United States on permanent paper.

British Library Cataloguing in Publication Data available

Library of Congress Cataloging in Publication Data

Makepeace, Joanna.
    Divine son of Ra / Joanna Makepeace.
      p.    cm.
    ISBN 0-7838-2016-X (lg. print : sc)
    1. Large type books.   I. Title.
    [PR6063.A359D58   1997]
    823'.914—dc21
                                          96-45130

To my mother
EDITH E. YORK
whose love and encouragement have
made this possible

# AUTHOR'S NOTE

All characters and events in this story are entirely fictitious. No effort has been made to draw a biographical account of any Pharaoh who may bear the name of Mern-ptah or Rameses.

# PART I

# 1

Serana shaded her eyes against the intense glare of the sun. She turned into the tent and began to busy herself with the preparation of food. She was so intent on her task that she did not hear Raban approach and she gave a startled little cry when his shadow darkened the tent flap. He smiled and throwing himself down on the pile of sheepskins, he gave a grunt of satisfaction as he kicked off his sandals. She hurried to bring him a bowl of goats' milk, meat, dates, bread and cheese, and he was silent for a while as he ate.

'Are the pack mules secured and watered?' she asked. He nodded, 'Yes and father is superintending the setting up of the other tents. He will come in soon.'

She half rose. 'He will want water.'

'Not yet. Sit down, sister, and eat. Once he is come there will be time for nothing but waiting on him.'

'Which means you want me to talk.'

He nodded, smiling, as he wiped his sticky fingers on the cloth she handed him. 'It has been a successful expedition. The price for wool was high.'

'How long before we reach the herd?' she said.

'Two . . . three days. We are following the Egyptian trade route. We leave the caravan to-morrow and strike off on our own.'

'Yes,' her sigh was almost imperceptible.

'You will regret it?'

'Why should I?'

He laughed, 'Oh little sister, am I blind that I do not notice the attentions of Ischian?'

'Oh,' she turned away to pour more milk for herself.

'You like him?'

'Well enough.'

'Well enough she says. He is the first-born of Sheik Ben Ismiel and very wealthy — and he admires you. That is obvious.'

'It is for father to decide.'

'He will not force you against your will, I think.'

'No, I think he will not. Our father loves me.'

She smiled suddenly and reached for his empty bowl. 'In this I am fortunate. Many girls of my age have no choice at all.'

'And what will you say if Ischian asks for you? He may well — tonight.'

'I do not know.' She flushed. 'What do you think of him, Raban?'

He stood up and turned away to the tent flap. 'I think him strong, forthright and honest and I wish him a thousand leagues away from my sister, for I do not wish to lose her so soon.'

'Dear Raban,' she stood up quickly and went to him. 'I do not know what to do. I'm only fifteen. There is time.'

He shook his head. 'Ischian is impatient for his bride. Father will be anxious to see you well provided for. I must be content, for he will be a good husband and considerate.'

She stepped out of the tent to the cooking pot on the fire of dried camel dung. She was the only woman in the train. Her father had given way to her pleading and allowed her to accompany himself and Raban to the wool sale at Ezion Geber. Now they followed the Egyptian trade route with the caravan and tomorrow they would leave it and strike off to the south to their own main encampment near Sinai.

She bent her head modestly as her father came over to the tent followed by the familiar tall figure of Ischian Ben Ismiel. They entered and she gave her attention to the potage, a flush dyeing her cheeks. She had noted Ischian Ben Ismiel's admiring glances, and Raban's remarks had further disturbed her. Soon she must leave her father's tents and cleave to her husband. For a year now, her father had spoken of her marriage portion. He was a wealthy man and she would take a fine dowry in herds and gold and silver with her.

Serana was the child of a strange wild barbarian woman from the northern coasts of The Great Sea. On one of his journeys, her father had bought her from Phoenician traders and given her all of his heart. She had borne him one child, Serana, and died in childbed and her little one had won the heart of the lonely man and his son by an earlier marriage.

They pampered and spoilt the gay child with the unusual pale complexion whose mane of hair was the colour of spun flax and whose eyes were as blue as the cloudless desert sky. This strange colouring had now won her admiring glances from the young men of the caravan train, and her pale hair, showing just one smooth band under her veil, had excited the attention of the young sheik who now sat within the tent with her father and brother.

She thought hard as she stirred the cooking pot. She would have to decide soon but did not know what to say. She admired the young man and he seemed both kindly and considerate but she knew nothing of what marriage entailed, only that she must leave her home, where she was petted and admired, to be the attentive wife of a man she hardly knew.

Vaguely she felt that there was under the surface, something distasteful and frightening in this being given in marriage, yet she knew that to be admired and in demand, was honourable and when her father spoke of her mother, which was rarely, it was in tones of mingled adoration and sadness. If he had loved her strange wild mother so greatly, what had she to fear now she too was admired and loved by this young wealthy tribesman? Her fierce love for her half brother Raban, made her hesitate before she made any decision about her answer. She loved Raban jealously and possessively. She dreaded the day she must leave his protective gentleness for ever.

She sighed softly as she carried in food to the two men and served them silently. Ischian's burning gaze followed her and his fingers sought and held hers for a moment as she handed him a bowl of goats' milk. She retired to the back of the tent at the close of the meal and picked up a robe she was embellishing with beads and coins. She was conscious of Ben Ismiel's attempts to keep her within his view as she sat well back in the shadows and she smiled a little.

The three men talked of the shearing and Raban questioned Ischian about Egypt where he had recently travelled.

'The Nile Lands are fertile and beautiful and the people seem free and happy enough among their vineyards and gardens. The townspeople live in luxury unheard of to us poor dwellers in the wilderness.'

Her father grunted. 'And what of the idol-filled temples?'

Ischian shook his head and said nothing and Raban continued. 'Is not Pharaoh considered as a god?'

'Yes that is so, almighty son of the sun-god, of royal and divine lineage. When I visited Thebes, I would have liked to catch a glimpse of him, but I did not. He remains secluded in his palace they say, since the death of the child.'

'Was it not his first-born?'

'Yes, three years ago a great plague swept Egypt and many died.'

The men had finished their talk. The young sheik gave thanks for her father's hospitality. Marack Ben Zareth stood up, a majestic figure in spite of encroaching age, he was over seventy, to bid his visitor farewell and went out with him into the night.

Marack Ben Zareth called Serana to him when he returned. He took her hands in his own and looked intently into her eyes.

'You like the young man, little one?'

'Yes, father,' she said quietly.

'Enough to leave your father's tents?'

'I do not know. He asked for me?'

He sighed and dropping her hands, turned away. 'Aye, he asked for you. He loves you greatly and longs to take you into his home.'

'You wish me to marry this man, my father?'

'Serana, you have been the light of my life and the comforter of my old age. I cannot bring myself to part with you though it is a fine match and he will deal well with you.' He turned back to her, a little smile twitching his lips. 'I have promised that if it is your wish — and not unless — you shall be his wife, but . . .' he shook his head as she tried to speak, 'not yet, not yet, my child. In a year perhaps if it is your will, then Raban shall take you to his tents. Are you content?'

Glad tears welled in her eyes and she covered his gnarled hands with kisses. 'All is well with me, my father. I am content.'

He gave her shoulders a light push. 'Then sleep,

my child, for we make an early start in the morning.'

Ischian came to Serana's side the following morning while she was gathering up the cooking vessels, preparatory to their departure from the caravan. He was to go on west to his home near Marah, while she and her father and Raban were to strike off south. He looked very grave as he bade her farewell. For the first time she let him hold her hands within his own.

'Your father told you I asked for you?' he said, as she lowered her head.

She nodded.

'I cannot bear to leave you for I love you, Serana. I will love no other as I desire you, you are like water in the desert and I shall thirst for you until you come to me. May I hope?'

Again she nodded, keeping her head lowered to hide her flush. 'Yes, Ischian, I think you may.'

His fingers gripped hers strongly and his voice was full of gladness. 'Then I will be patient, but do not make me wait too long.'

Gently he disengaged his fingers and lifted her face to his. 'I promise,' she said quietly, 'I will come to you within the year or not at all.'

He reached out to detain her but Raban came over and his hand fell back.

'Ready, Serana?' her brother enquired.

'Yes.'

'Then we must start. We hope to reach the tents of Hazeer before nightfall.'

'You visit Hazeer then?' Ischian said. 'I saw

the wily old fox two moons ago. He was rejoicing in once more evading Pharaoh's tax collectors. One day they'll catch up with him.'

'We camp with him for the night,' Raban said. 'He is a cousin of my father's.'

Ischian said then, more seriously, 'You know your sister's mind, Raban?'

'Aye, I know it, though I dread to lose her, I will bring her to your tent gladly, when she is ready.'

'Then I am satisfied,' Ischian said, and bidding them farewell, he strode off to the waiting camels.

Raban watched his sister intently as she followed him with her eyes, then he shook her shoulder gently. 'Hasten little one, our father waits.'

They were greeted by Hazeer gladly. It was late by the time they made camp and Serana was glad to allow Hazeer's servants to wait upon her. Hazeer, her father's cousin, was an old man but he had a young concubine, Zipanah, and it was pleasant to have feminine company again. Zipanah was delighted to hear of Serana's coming betrothal and talked animatedly of bridal clothes. When she finally retired, Serana was glad to stretch out on her couch and was soon asleep.

She slept soundly until just before dawn when she was awakened by the strange thundering sound. She yawned, and pushed back the covers and stretched. The sun was not yet up but already the household was stirring. She could hear women calling to one another and the agitated answers of men. She sat up suddenly, one hand pulling the bedcovers over her exposed breasts. Men rushed hurriedly by and confusion seemed all around her, then Raban tore aside the tent flap and shouted to her. 'Get up and get dressed.'

She stared at him stupefied. He strode over to the couch and shook her roughly. 'Did you hear me. Get up. I must go to father. Hurry now.'

A frightened servant stopped him outside and she heard Raban's curt instructions, then he tore off in the direction of their own tents and animals.

Hazeer stood in the centre of the encampment, behind him a group of terrified slaves and servants and the women of the household. About twenty yards away stood a line of Egyptian chariots, and in each a tall impassive spearman accompanied the driver.

Serana stared at them fascinated. Her gaze travelled from their simple white pleated kilts, bare chests and striped headdresses. Their faces seemed hewn out of stone. Not a smile or sign of excitement gleamed in the whole line. The sun glinted on their weapons and one of the horses reared impatiently and was quickly curbed by the driver.

One of the Egyptians stepped down from his chariot and walked to meet Hazeer. He too was simply dressed but he wore a heavy gold necklace and bracelet. Evidently he was someone of rank and importance. In silence, he crossed the space

17

which separated him from Hazeer and began to speak with him. Serana could not catch what was said. She understood the Egyptian tongue but the two were too far away for her to get the import of their talk.

Hazeer's voice rose in anger. He waved his arms expressively. The other remained calm and answered in quick, crisp tones. Serana gave a little cry of surprise as her shoulder was grasped from behind and turning, saw Raban.

'What is wrong? Is the fool refusing to pay? This is Pharaoh's Sinai tax collector.'

'I don't know, I can't hear but they don't appear to agree. Surely he has the tribute.'

'He must have. He knew in the end he would have to pay. Nothing can withstand Pharaoh's armies when they move.'

'Where is father?'

'Within the tent. He is dressed and ready.'

Suddenly Hazeer turned away from the official tax collector and moved towards his household. He walked as an old man. The official moved unhurriedly back to the watchful charioteers and rapped out an order.

Serana saw her father go across to the old sheik. He caught his old comrade in his arms and they spoke together for some moments. Hazeer's two sons then took their father and guided him into the tent. He seemed still inclined to argue but the elder one was insistent and they passed inside.

'He goes to fetch the tribute,' Marack said as

Raban looked at him questioningly. 'But this is not all. The tax collector demands his elder son as hostage. The old man has offered to pay twice the tribute due, but he refuses. The boy must go.'

'Oh no,' Serana cried.

'They'll not harm him,' Raban said quietly. 'He's just a guarantee to make sure the old fox pays up next time without fuss. In time they'll probably allow him to return. Meanwhile, he'll eat his heart out in captivity. The old man is heart-broken, knowing it's all his fault.'

The household servants had received their instructions. They scurried about and soon the tribute sacks were brought out and their contents revealed for the inspection of the tax collector. Hazeer's tent flap was thrown aside as he came out with his two sons. Caleb, the elder, embraced his father then walked over to Raban and Marack who wished him a safe journey. He spoke to his household servants, two of whom were weeping, then moved to join the impassive stern-faced official.

Just how it happened Serana never knew, that action that brought horror and disaster into her life. One moment the encampment seemed quiet and still, the next, there was noise and confusion. As the young man reached the Egyptian's side, there was a sudden twanging sound. The Egyptian gave a gurgling scream and dropped in his tracks, an arrow transfixing his throat. For one split second everyone stood still, staring horror stricken, then all hell was let loose. Raban tore his sister back to the tent as the Egyptian chariots charged. Women and children screamed. Animals ran about in terror. Tent poles snapped under the sudden attack. Men fought hand over hand. Where there had been peace, agony was all she could sense. Raban left her side and she clung to the ridge pole, sick with horror. Zipanah flew by screaming with an Egyptian soldier hot in pursuit. A small child crawled to her side, blood darkening his robe and lay still.

How long it lasted she did not know. She bent down over the child while the conflict raged all round her. She knew he was dead, Zipanah's only son. She stood up and began to thread her way through the carnage.

The Egyptians were now rounding up the servants. All revolt was soon crushed. The little nomad community had no weapons, was unprepared and ill equipped. All around lay the bodies of the dead and dying. In an agony of fear Serana sought her father and brother.

She found her father face down on the floor of his tent. She called his name and lifted him on to his back. It was then that she saw the ominous dark stain on his robe. She whispered to him brokenly. A glazed stare was her only answer. How long she sat cradling his body in her arms she could not tell. Raban found her and lifted his father's weight from her arms.

'Let me have him, little one,' he said quietly.

She allowed him to take the body without resistance. Then at last it came, terrible silent screams which stuck in her throat and allowed no sound to issue forth. He called her name, shook her, but to no avail. She neither saw nor heard him. She was alone in the agony of her grief. She did not even realise an Egyptian soldier had strode roughly into the tent, seized Raban and bound his arms. When an officer followed him in and took in the situation, he bent down and lifted her into his strong arms.

Only then did she come out of her stupor to hear Raban's shout of rage and frustration. She struggled weakly in the arms of her captor, then fell back, and blackness mercifully engulfed her.

# 2

Ashtar drew her fingers across the strings in a last mournful little chord. She placed the small lyre quietly at her side. The man by the colonnade did not turn, he did not even stir. He sat quite still, his thoughts abstracted.

It was two years since the Syrian king, her father, had given her as a gift to Pharaoh, two years since she had lived at court and been concubine to the man she was now watching. Her brow contracted slightly in anxiety. Among all his women she alone knew his strange arrogant nature and pitied him. She had prepared herself to hate this man with all the savage pent-up passion latent in her. To be given like this, as one gives gold or animals as a bribe. She had sobbed and pleaded, screamed herself into a passion, but it had availed her nothing. To Thebes she had come, richly clothed and endowed like so much baggage as a free will offering to tempt the favour of Pharaoh. She had won his favour indeed.

Ashtar was beautiful. She was now approaching eighteen and in the full flower of her womanhood, tall above the average her body had fulfilled the promise of girlhood and blossomed to ripe perfection. Her proud dusky face glowed with the power of her intense passionate nature. Her hair was dressed to perfection and oiled into sleek gold plaits, her lids shaded with malachite and her beautiful lambent eyes enriched by the skilled application of kohl. They carried now a hint of sadness and uncertainty, as she watched her lord.

Pharaoh had a strange difficult nature. She had arrived at court shortly after the divorce of his queen and consort Nefertari. This had followed on the death of his only child, and in the warmth of her vibrant nature she had tried to comfort him. Almost at once, she sensed the agony of loss which prompted the outbreaks of petulance and displays of arrogance. She glimpsed, with a shrewd, discerning woman's eyes, the man naked and unadorned under the panoply and regalia of the Divine Son of Ra. She had prayed to the gods for a child to comfort his loneliness, but her prayers remained unanswered. He petted and spoiled her, was pleased by her skilled lovemaking but she knew he did not love her. He consulted her when he needed advice, sought her when depressed or angry. He had come to her apartment two hours ago and thrown himself on to the long seat near the colonnade and curtly ordered her to play to him. Now she sat silent, awaiting his pleasure. Suddenly her fingers caught unawares the strings of the exquisite little instrument, making a discordant jangling sound, and on the instant, he turned abruptly to face her.

23

'I crave your forgiveness, Ashtar, I neglect you. My thoughts were miles away.'

'Something saddens my lord?'

'No, I am not sad,' he said, 'only rather thoughtful and tired.' I expect news from Punt. The messengers are overdue. I also received information this morning that one of my tax collectors had been killed while obtaining a hostage. The cavalry detachment dealt summarily with the offenders and have taken slaves and booty in plenty.' He frowned, 'Nevertheless this is very disturbing. I must tighten up this procedure.'

Broad shouldered and slim hipped, he was a tall regal figure, towering over her, one hand idly playing with a jewelled bracelet on his forearm. This afternoon, he wore only a short pleated tunic of green linen, and soft leather sandals. His fierce black eyes were unusually softened and the wonted heavy scowl was absent from his features. The crown was laid aside with his ceremonial beard, yet Ramoses still made a dominating figure. Ashtar noted the arrogant, finely chiselled features and the lips, which were too beautiful for a man. This mobile generous mouth betrayed sensitivity, which she knew lay under the surface.

He stopped fiddling with the golden arm ornament and looked up as the gardener's boy walked by the fish pond, a short, sturdy figure of about seven years. Ashtar's gaze did not miss the sudden yearning which darkened the royal eyes and she sat up and swiftly touched his bare shoulder.

'The gods will give you a son, lord. Have faith.'

'The gods,' he swung round on her angrily, his black eyes flashing fury, so that she drew back abashed, 'speak not to me of the gods. They are but a superstition to frighten simpletons and children.'

She did not attempt to argue but decided to change the subject. 'The Nubian woman who arrived from the market, she amuses you?'

He shrugged and sat down beside her on the day bed. 'She interested me for a while, now I tire of her. Her mind is that of a small child. She wants only petting and bright clothing and jewels.' His fingers reached out and touched her hair. Unlike you, Ashtar, she has no wisdom or understanding to soothe my jangling thoughts. You will ever be my favourite.'

'The woman who gives you a son will take my place. Pray the gods it will be soon. You know you treat your women like dolls, yes even me. You pamper and spoil them, shower them with gew-gaws . . . I sometimes think . . . I . . .' She broke off with a sudden laugh of embarrassment and he prompted her.

'You think?'

'Nothing.' She stood up and moved to her toilet table and picking up a bronze mirror, scrutinised her lovely face intently.

He smiled broadly and lay back on the bed surveying her as she repaired one or two defects discovered in her appearance. 'You mean I should play the conqueror and take what is mine by force.'

'I did not say that,' she swung round, alarmed.

'You did not say it but you implied it. Perhaps you are right. Maybe I should take your advice and begin with yourself. Would the height of my passion compare with that of Rehoremheb's.'

The alabaster box of eye paint fell from her hands to lie in pieces on the floor while white to the lips, she stood staring at him. His lips curved into a deeper smile while his eyes mocked her. Unmoving, she stood, only her eyes showed the full dawning horror of her fear. It seemed an eternity before he broke the silence with a short sharp laugh.

'You have no need to fear, my lovely Ashtar. Your secret is safe.'

'You know?'

'I have known for months.'

She moved forward and dropping to her knees, seized his hands and covered them with kisses, then she began to sob, brokenly. 'I love him, lord. We couldn't help it. I didn't want it to happen. I tried so hard to stop it. Did you think I didn't care about his safety as well as my own. There were times when my eyes yearned for the sight of him and my arms ached to hold him, but I wouldn't go to him or allow him near me.'

He caught her in his arms and lifted her on to the day bed. 'Hush Ashtar, quiet, do you want the attendants to hear?'

She stopped her anguished sobbing and stared at him for a long time without speaking. 'Don't you care?' she said at last.

He put her away from him with a little shrug. 'Why should I? I don't expect you to give your heart with your body. That wasn't included in your father's bargain.'

'And Rehoremheb? He will be safe . . .' she faltered, her eyes imploring him.

'Yes, but you must both be discreet.' He held her eyes with his own. 'You understand?'

She nodded tremulously.

'If this is known in court circles I cannot save you. I care only for my honour. If you defile that, I shall destroy both of you without the slightest compunction. I would give you your freedom if I could but that is out of the question.' He stood up and moved to the open doorway again and stood staring out over the garden. 'I love you, Ashtar. I wish I could give you your happiness as you have striven to give me mine, but this I cannot do. If I discard you, your father would consider it mortal insult, and it would be tantamount to a declaration of war. This I will not do. If you leave me, it will cry your shame the length and breadth of the Two Lands and the lives of both of you would not be worth a copper coin. If you love him, Ashtar, you will be sensible and send him away. If he is caught, the manner of his dying will be unthinkable.'

'I can't lord, I can't.'

He turned, 'Then I should, for your sake.'

His lips curled suddenly in a hard smile. 'For all your yielding flesh and gentle ways, you are all woman, Ashtar. What you want you take, even if you destroy all around you in the taking. No . . .' he waved her away, 'no . . . I'll not betray you and your lover. Where I can, I'll even protect you for I owe you something for the hours of peace I spend here.'

He moved to step out into the garden. 'The gods grant you peace, Ashtar.'

He did not look at her again but walked through the gardens to his own apartments. Nefren, his personal attendant, rose silently as he approached and without a word, assisted him to disrobe. He threw himself into the sunken bath and scrubbed away at his flesh as if he would scour away with it, his fears for Ashtar. Nefren sensed his mood and moved about his tasks silently and skilfully. Ramoses lay back on the limestone slab, while his slave anointed his body with sweet smelling oils. He watched the man with half-closed eyes.

Nefren had been captured in a raid to the south. At first he had been rebellious and his arrogance, as fierce as Pharoah's own, had only been subdued by the lash and the threat of further torment. It had been interesting to watch whether pain and fear could conquer pride. Seemingly it had. Nefren was attentive and no longer mutinous and yet Ramoses wondered. Did he bide his time? Would he still plunge his dagger into Pharaoh's unprotected back if the opportunity offered itself? It had been a pleasurable thrill to risk his life in the other's hands, to note the subdued glance blaze occasionally with frustrated fury. Today there was no flicker of hatred in the quiet gaze as Nefren clothed him in white, draped his heavy pectoral across his chest, and fastened on his be-jewelled sandals.

'Has the party from Sinai arrived at the palace?'

'Yes, lord. It awaits you in the great hall, also the messenger from Punt.'

'Good.' Pharaoh stood up as the other held out the crown. He gazed at his reflection in the bronze mirror the slave held for him. Now he was clothed in the might and majesty of Egypt. Only thus did he feel secure. The power he wielded gave him some satisfaction and he nodded content, taking into his hands the sacred crook and flail.

'I have just left the Lady Ashtar,' he said deliberately. 'She needs protection when she leaves the palace and reliable bearers. See to it.'

Nefren veiled his eyes and bowed. He knew Pharaoh's heart as no other, and in his hands lay the safety of his master's favourite. He too was content to watch and wait.

# 3

Serana stood quite still staring at the great bronze doors which led into Pharaoh's hall of audience. Raban's eyes grew more and more anxious as he noted that vacant stare. It had become more pronounced during the days of that terrible journey to Thebes. She seemed empty, oblivious of all pain and fear, moving like an automaton. From his Egyptian captor, he had learned that slaves taken in battle were the property of Pharaoh, usually to be sold in the common market. This would probably happen in their case.

Never in his life had he glimpsed such magnificence as this outer hall. He stared entranced at the pillars of solid marble gilded and ornamented with the lotus design. Crowds of courtiers and members of the palace household swarmed the antechamber. Serana seemed not to notice. She looked down at the floor and when he moved to her side, as the great doors were thrown open, she did not even respond to the gentle, comforting pressure of his hand on her arm.

Their guards edged them forward into the hall of audience itself, towards the throne on the raised dais at the far end, where sat the stiff enthroned figure of the ruler of the Two Lands. Leaving them near to the doors, the officer marched quickly forward and saluting smartly, handed his scroll to the vizier who stood at the right hand of Pharaoh.

The great hall was heavy with myrrh and sandalwood. Above the throne, two huge Nubian slaves rhythmically wielded great fans of ostrich feathers. Ranged behind Pharaoh was a company of white-robed shaven-headed priests, courtiers and ladies of the court.

He sat like a statue, stiffly holding the crook and flail, listening to the report of his commander. The man prostrated himself and touched the ground before the feet of Pharaoh with his lips, then rose and moved back to the waiting slaves. He had handed over to the scribes his tally of coin and possessions. His mission was now complete. It needed now only the handing over of the slaves to the market. He signalled to the guards to lead out the captives, but Pharaoh's voice arrested him.

'Wait. The girl! Bring her to me.'

The officer glanced briefly at the huddled little group. There were three women in the company, two of Hazeer's household and the mad fair girl who had not spoken a word since the raid. He hesitated for a fraction of a moment.

'The one who has yellow hair.'

It was the mad woman Pharaoh had noted. The officer was not surprised. The girl was certainly unusual. Her skin was of exceptional whiteness and that yellow hair was beautiful without doubt, but those eyes disturbed him. The girl had lost her senses and could be difficult. The brother too could be a problem. He had noted during the journey how he doted on her. The officer sighed. To hear Pharaoh was to obey. He spoke to the girl.

'Here you, come with me.'

She stared at him wonderingly in that childlike witless way and the brother moved and placed himself protectively in front of her. The officer motioned to one of the guards who forced him back, imprisoning his hands behind his back. The young captive struggled helplessly in his grasp and the officer led the girl unresistingly towards the dias to stand before the face of Pharaoh.

It seemed to Serana that the sight of this majestic awe-inspiring figure was the first thing to impress itself upon her returning senses. The throne and its proud occupant loomed before her. She was conscious of the arrogant stare of two fierce black eyes appraising her, of high cheek bones and dominating chin, then beneath, a shimmer of gold and turquoise and bare flesh.

The great hall with its brightly painted pillars seemed to close in on her and the dazzling, garishly dressed people appeared to advance and recede before her vision, but she pulled herself sharply together. The Egyptian captain was speaking to her.

'Prostrate yourself before the might of Pharaoh.'

Fear made her voice shrill. 'I will not kneel before the murderer of my father.'

A flicker of interest gleamed in the eyes of Pharaoh. The girl had spirit. She was afraid; he sensed it in the tense rigidity of her body poise and the sudden tightening of the lips, but her strange light eyes stared boldly back into his own. He was used to women crawling to sue for his favour. This was a new experience.

'So you are the daughter of this Hazeer who defied me and caused the death of my official.'

'No, I am the daughter of Marack Ben Zareth and that is my brother Raban. We are not responsible for the death of your tax collector. We were at Hazeer's tents on a visit. I demand that you set us free.'

A little buzz went up from the assembled court. Pharaoh held up his hand for silence. 'You are a relative of Hazeer?'

'My father was his cousin.'

A slight smile played around the lips of Pharaoh. He motioned to his officer.

'Kneel, girl,' the man commanded, 'it is the custom. You stand before the great son of Ra himself. Pharaoh is descended from the gods.'

Serana did not answer nor did she move to obey. Once more Pharaoh gave a slight lift of the chin and the man seized her and threw her down before his feet. With a snarl of rage Raban wrenched himself from the restraining arms of his guard and launched himself at the figure on the throne. A great gasp went up from the assembled court. Completely taken by surprise, it was some seconds before anyone came to Pharaoh's assistance, but Ramoses had been trained in the wrestling ring as a youth with the other princes and he had not lost his skill. As the infuriated youth threw himself at him, he stepped lightly aside, and seized him in an agonising lock. Raban gave a scream of pain as he felt his arms almost torn from their sockets.

As Pharaoh turned, Serana sprang at him like a wildcat. The young captain had relaxed his grip on her in the suddenness of the attack on Pharaoh and she clawed at his bared upper arms screaming with fear and fury. He released Raban, caught her hands and held them in a tight grip, conscious of the pain where her nails had torn his flesh. She was held at arm's length helpless, while his smile deepened and grew ever more cruel.

'Very lovely,' he said quietly, 'very very lovely and most rare — but so ill mannered. We must teach you both better manners. Take her.'

The captain took her by the shoulders and held her firmly. All her pent-up fury had now evaporated and she stood quiescent in his grip.

'Take them away,' Pharaoh commanded. 'Bring them to my apartments in an hour, both of them.' His eyes glinted strangely as the captives were hustled down the length of the hall of audience and away.

He dusted down his disarranged kilt and settled the glittering winged disc on his chest, then still smiling, resumed his stiff position on the throne.

'Now I will receive the messengers from Punt,' he said quietly, 'admit them.'

# 4

Men-ophar, the Egyptian captain, glanced sym-pathetically at the fair slave as she sat huddled in a corner of the guard room. Once over that fatal outburst, she seemed as tractable as ever she had been during the journey to the capital. There were no tears or appeals for assistance, not even questions. She sat gazing at the earthen floor her hands twisting and untwisting in cease-less misery.

He walked over to the table where his men gossiped and ate and brought over to the girl a jug of honey wine, some cheese and bread. She looked up at him wonderingly and shook her head.

'You must eat. You will need your strength.'

'Thank you, captain. I will eat a little bread to please you, if you insist.'

He watched gratified as she crumbled the bread nervously and consumed a little.

'My brother?' she whispered, 'can you tell me of him?'

'He is under guard. No harm has come to him — yet.'

She turned to face him, searching his impassive face for some glimpse of hope to comfort her and he bent to pick up the food vessels, unable to face the sick dread in her eyes.

'They will kill him,' she said at last.

He shrugged. 'To lay violent hands on Pharaoh is punishable by death. He might yet live. To live is to hope.'

'But you do not believe there is any.'

'I did not say so. There are the mines and the brick pits. You must hope and pray to your god with all your heart.'

A servant came to the door of the guard room. The captain rose and went to him. She guessed what was said, though she heard no words. Menophar spoke awkwardly, embarrassed pity making his voice harsh. 'You will not be foolish?'

She shook her head and he led her through the corridors of the palace to a room at its rear.

Pharaoh's apartments were light and airy, the furniture tasteful and serviceable. Ramoses was a soldier as well as a ruler and his room echoed in its simplicity, his need for the practical and useful around him. One wall was open to the garden letting in the heavy night scent of the flowers and shrubs. The others were painted brightly with frescoes of scenes along the Nile bank. There was nothing to jar or irritate the sensitivity of eye in this pleasant airy room yet Serana shivered involuntarily, as she entered.

Pharaoh stood, arms akimbo, awaiting her and she faltered as she saw her brother standing submissively between two guards.

'Welcome, daughter of Marack,' Pharaoh said

mockingly. 'We were awaiting you.' He indicated a carved chair to his right. 'Be seated.'

Her eyes flickered nervously from his tall commanding form, devoid now of its ceremonial robes and dressed comfortably in a single garment of blue linen, to that of her brother. She glanced at the throne-like chair and stepped back a little.

'Disobedient too, I see.' He snapped his fingers impatiently and the captain pushed her gently into the seat, taking his place behind her.

'So,' Pharaoh's eyes regarded her coolly, 'you are seated, I am not ill-mannered, daughter of the wilderness, I do not attack my guests,' he paused smiling, 'not yet, at any rate.'

She closed her eyes as faintness swept over her and she fought it back. She could not play the coward now and shame Raban. She looked at her brother appealingly. He smiled back at her, striving to give her confidence, though his eyes showed his fears for her and his lips trembled at his inability to aid her.

'Nefren, summon my Nubians,' Pharaoh spoke without turning his head, his eyes still watching Serana and the slave struck the small gong behind him. He stood in the shadows watching this scene, a perplexed frown darkening his brow.

Pharaoh was in a royal rage. He noted it in the tension of his body and the silky soft notes of his voice. It boded ill for the tall Bedouin youth, but the girl . . . Nefren looked at her admiringly. Even in this agony of fear she was beautiful. Pharaoh was speaking again, softly, mockingly.

'Did your father not teach you manners, little one? Did he not instruct you to bow submissively before your menfolk, or is this not the custom among your people? Surely, I misunderstood, for I heard Bedouin women were obedient.'

'To their husbands, yes that is so,' she answered softly, her mouth dry.

'To their masters?'

She did not answer. Her trapped gaze attempted to avoid his but was caught and held by his own. 'Their masters?' he repeated.

'Yes.' Her voice was so low that he but guessed at her reply. 'I understand now that I must obey. I will obey . . . only . . .' her voice broke in a sob, 'only spare my brother.'

His smile broadened. 'Ah yes, the brother,' and turning his black eyes swept over Raban's taut body. 'Yes, we must not forget the brother.'

In answer to his summons, two huge Negroes now entered the room, the light of the lamps flickering over the smooth ebony of their massive forms. He indicated Raban and spoke commandingly, 'Secure him to the pillar.'

Speechless with terror, Serana watched as her brother was seized and his hands deftly lashed together, while the other Black fastened him to the pillar. Pharaoh's eyes watched her as her own eyes widened with dread. It was when the bigger of the two produced a huge whip of rhinoceros hide and uncoiled it, that she burst from the captain's restraining hands and fell on her face at his feet.

'No no, please not that, not that.'

Pharaoh made no answer. His eyes glittered as he surveyed her heaving shoulders with the wealth of hair like spun gold falling on his feet in a soft cloud.

'Thrash me. It was my foolish pride that was at fault.'

He looked back at her coolly. 'You must be patient, little one, your turn will come.'

Her lips parted suddenly soundlessly and Menophar lifted her away and carried her to the seat.

She could not take her eyes from her brother. The Nubian lifted the great whip and at a signal from Pharaoh, brought it down across her brother's chest. In spite of his determination to take this unflinchingly, a sharp cry of agony burst from his lips, as the white hot pain slashed his flesh. Again and again the whip rose and fell. Too horror-stricken even to scream, Serana covered her ears and turned away from the sight, sick with horror. The first shock over, he made no further outcries. His teeth came down savagely on to his bottom lip and he tasted the salt blood fresh on his mouth and tensed his body to withstand the force of the blows. Blackness hovered about his consciousness like a heavy cloud. He fought it off, striving to spare his sister the sight of his swooning body. How pleasant it would be to pass away into this engulfing blackness, yet he held his mind grimly on and on . . .

Suddenly it was over. Serana could not understand why the heavy sound of blows had stopped. Seized with dread, she turned to find her brother slumped against the pillar while the two Blacks released him and supported his nerveless weight.

'So,' Pharaoh's voice sounded cool, unmoved. 'Take him to the guard-house. Tomorrow, I will consider what is to be done with him.'

She reached out imploring hands towards him as the two Nubians half carried, half dragged him from the room, but she was firmly held back by her captor. Pharaoh turned towards her.

'One lesson partly learned. He has fortitude this brother of yours, what of you, his sister?'

For the first time she became aware of the attendant standing in the shadows. Pharaoh motioned him towards the chair and Nefren and one of the soldiers lifted her and drew her to the pillar. Half fainting she felt herself fastened to it, this time with her back to Pharaoh and her face smudged and swollen with tears, pressed to its decorated column. Dimly she was aware of Pharaoh moving to her side. She smelt the sweet fragrance of his body oil. He was silent for a moment and it seemed an eternity before he spoke. 'You are my slave, my property to use or dispose of as I please,' he said at last. It may be my pleasure to keep you, but keep you or not, I will teach you obedience. I think you understand.' He stepped back a pace. 'Nefren, my chariot whip.'

She hardly felt the pain although it was considerable. Humiliation and fear for Raban made her oblivious to everything that was happening. Vaguely, she heard the tearing sound her robe made, as Nefren ripped it from her back and then she felt the sudden sting of the slender whip Pharaoh himself wielded. Tears blinded her eyes but she wept not for herself but her brother, pleading with the god she hardly recognised, to save him from his fate.

Nefren released her and lifted her into his arms. Pharaoh tossed the blood-stained whip from him and wiped his hands clean on a linen kerchief.

'Let the women bathe and clothe her and bring her to me,' he said curtly, then turning, he walked out into the garden.

Nefren bore the fainting girl to the bath house and summoned attendants. He laid her down on the bathing slab and sprinkled water on her face. She opened her eyes and looked up at him, while his own brown ones took in her pitiful condition. Her eyes darted round the room and she drew back as three slave women approached. 'These women will attend you. They will be gentle. Let them bathe and anoint your wounds. I will come for you.'

She sprang to a crouching position and drew away from them. 'No, I will not. Stay away from me.' The women drew together into a group and eyed her nervously.

'Don't be foolish,' he said tonelessly, 'you have no choice. Did you not hear Pharaoh? You are his slave, his property. It is not for you to say what you will or will not do.' He moved towards her and she sprang at him raking her nails down his cheek. With a muttered oath he sprang back, his hand to his injured face. 'Daughter of Sekmet,' he said angrily, 'do you force me to hold you still for them?' As she did not answer, he seized her hands. 'Be not so foolish. What do you think this will gain you? I have told you, you can do nothing but submit.' With all her strength she tried to free herself from his grip, then suddenly she collapsed into agonised weeping. He patted her torn shoulder gently.

'There, that is better, cry a little. Relieve your overfull heart. Do you think I do not pity you? Only let the women do their work. They will be beaten if they do not obey orders. You don't wish that?' She shook her head but the anguished weeping continued. He beckoned the waiting women forward. 'Attire her for Pharaoh's bed. She needs healing salve for her back. Fetch it, one of you. She will be quiet now.'

'No,' the word was shouted defiantly, 'I will not submit, I will kill myself with my bare hands first.' She wrenched herself free from him and retreated back against the far wall. One woman hurried for the salve; the other two stopped short, their eyes on Nefren.

He hesitated then drew his bronze hunting knife and stepped towards her. 'Destroy yourself then. I'll make it easy for you but think — you leave your brother to face Pharaoh's fury alone.'

The knife dropped from her fingers and she buried her face in her hands. 'Oh my God, why do you allow this,' she whimpered, 'what have we done that you leave us comfortless?'

He stooped and picked up the discarded weapon. 'Come now you must not distress yourself. This is not the end of the world. Are you the first woman to be taken against her will? In Pharaoh's arms you will be no worse off than in any other's. A hundred women would give half their lives to change positions with you tonight. Pharaoh has thirty women in his palace. He will perhaps tire of you after tonight, but if you are sensible you will try to please him. Remember your brother still lives, his fate lies in Pharaoh's hands. He may even let him live if only to torture you with uncertainty. If you take your life he will have no such chance.'

His counsel was good and she knew it. She sank down on the slab without further resistance. She was only half conscious of the women's skilful fingers as they disrobed her and gently laved her body, rubbing healing salve into the lash wounds and anointing her pale skin with sweet-smelling oil. She was not even aware of Nefren's continued presence, though never once before had a man seen her naked form. If she had been aware of it, she would not have cared. What else mattered now? She had known all humiliation in this dread place.

The women twittered as they washed and dried her bright hair, combed it into damp unrestrained

44

waves on to her shoulders and clothed her in transparent linen.

Nefren caught his breath at her beauty, as she stood ready to go with him. The quality of her sorrow seemed only to heighten her loveliness. He took her by the hand and led her to Pharaoh's sleeping chamber, then gently he pushed her inside and left her.

# 5

A noisy throng of women was bathing in the largest of the palace pools. The sun stood high in the heavens and was pouring down remorselessly on the palace and its environs but Serana shivered and drew her almost transparent over-robe tightly across her breasts. One of the women, bronzed and dark-eyed, called to her, inviting her to join them in the water, but she ignored the summons and turned from them. A group of watchful slaves waited to attend them some paces off and two fat eunuchs kept wary eyes on their charges.

Serana walked towards an opening in the garden fence. No one made a move to stop her and she felt she must get away from the constant chatter and rest her aching head. She passed under a shaded arbor into another garden where gardeners clad only in short loose loin cloths were busy cutting back the shrubs and watering the seedling plants.

She tried not to think upon the horror of the night she had spent in the arms of Pharaoh. She shuddered and tried to shut out the memory of his mocking taunts. Nefren had counselled her

and would be destined to eat out their hearts in loneliness year after year, until death brought them release. He cast a final glance at the lovely girl who had aroused his pity and hurried on. He would be late for his audience.

Serana did not notice the tall fine figure of the priest, nor was she aware of the wealth of his pity. She was shut away in the tomb of her own sorrow. She stumbled on, anxious to find somewhere dark and quiet where she could hide herself like an animal away from the curious stares and respectful salutes of court attendants and slaves. She found it at last, in a small secluded enclosure. She passed through a wooden gate into a courtyard surrounded by high brick walls against which grew vines and small trees. It was quite empty and silent, only the sound of water bubbling into a small ornamental pond from a small central jet, broke its stillness. Serana closed the gate behind her and leaned against it. For a few blessed moments, she could be alone. Invisible hammers beat in her brain and now her body seemed on fire. She staggered towards the pool and laved her heated forehead and breast. The water was cool and refreshing. She half lay, half sat on the coping, then suddenly in the quiet peace of the place, the dam which she had imposed on her feelings the night before, gave, and she broke into a passionate storm of weeping. It was here that Ashtar, returning to her apartments after shopping in the city, found her.

'My dear,' she said, 'Can I help you?'

49

Serana shook her head, dashing away the tears with her bare arm. 'I'm sorry, lady,' she whispered, 'I should not be here. I crave your pardon. It seemed so quiet.'

Ashtar touched her arm and recoiled at its hot burning dryness. She called briskly to her women and pulled Serana to her feet.

'You are ill. Your body is fevered. Come into the palace and rest.'

'No, no,' Serana drew away, wary of trusting herself to this lovely but wealthy stranger.

'You must,' Ashtar indicated the dripping garment which had fallen forward into the water. 'This must be removed. It is wet and will increase your body chill, thus furthering the fever.'

Protesting weakly, Serana was half carried half dragged into the cool interior of the favourite's apartments. Here Ashtar sent her women for scented water, towels and blankets. Between them, the women undressed Serana and wrapped her in warm blankets. Ashtar exclaimed over her wounded back.

'Who has mistreated you so? If it is an overseer, he shall be punished.' She gently drew the terrified girl into her sleeping chamber and assisted her on to the bed. 'You must rest and keep warm. When you wake you can tell me what is wrong. No,' she held up a deprecating finger as Serana tried to still her chattering teeth to explain, 'not now. Later will be soon enough. Sala, fetch me the fever draught I had from the priests a week ago.'

Tears came readily to Serana's eyes though the bitter weeping had now stilled. She still felt deadly cold and the soft home-spun blankets were warm to her body, which seemed unaccountably hot and cold by turns, and she clutched them round her, frightened eyes following her benefactress as she moved round the room. How lovely she was in her sheath-like silver dress. Her presence made Serana feel safe, for the first time since she had arrived in Egypt. She allowed herself the luxury of silent tears with no restraint. The older woman did not try to stop her. When the woman came back with a bowl of colourless fluid, she herself brought it to Serana and coaxed her to drink.

'Take this. It will ease the fever and let you rest. The liquid is quite harmless.'

Serana found it rather bitter, but not unpleasant. It quenched her burning thirst and she drained the bowl gratefully.

'There you see, you can trust me. Nothing can be worth this terrible weeping. Sleep and soon things will not appear so dreadful.'

She placed the bowl on a small stool by the bed and was about to stand up, when she heard Pharaoh's voice in the corridor. Serana heard it too. She sat upright and clutched at Ashtar. 'Oh Lady, do not tell him I am here. I pray you do not.'

Ashtar stared down at her, astonished. 'That is the voice of Pharaoh. He comes to visit me. Do not be afraid.'

'He will not come in here?'

'I promise he shall not. Does that satisfy you?' She stared at the girl's terror-stricken blue eyes, unable to gauge the reason for her alarm. This was not the effect Ramoses usually had on the women of the household. 'I have said you can trust me. Won't you?'

Serana looked into her dusky beautiful face. She seemed satisfied, as she gave a minute little nod and sank back, clutching the disarranged covering round her.

From the next room, Ashtar heard her attendants' soft voices as they answered Pharaoh's queries. She drew beaded curtains across the sleeping alcove, cast a final glance of reassurance at Serana, and stepped out into the outer room, to make her obeisance before Pharaoh.

He lifted her to her feet and gave a slightly amused laugh, 'You seem startled, my lovely Ashtar. Did I take you by surprise?'

She laughed softly in answer. 'I did not expect you, my lord. I heard you were to visit the Temple this morning. I thought I saw Ptah Hoten in the palace. There is nothing wrong at the Temple?'

'No, he brought plans for the new outbuildings. He plans to enlarge the Temple and make more grain bins. He feels if the Nile over-reaches its usual distance as it did at the last inundation, there will be many families homeless and he wishes to accommodate them in the Temple. It stands as high as the palace, and they will be safe there.'

She rose, and fetching wine, poured it into a cup of finely glazed ware. Crossing to his side with the wine, she noticed the deep scratches on his bare shoulder and made a little exclamation of dismay.

He laughed as he took the wine from her. 'Ah, you notice my war scars. They were made by a golden-haired wildcat Captain Men-ophar brought me from Sinai.' As she continued to look puzzled, he drained the cup and went on, 'She flew at me with her talons after her brother had to be forcibly restrained from attempting to kill me. He objected to the two of them being requested to bow to me.'

'How did they come here?'

'They are slaves found in the household of Hazeer. He refused to pay his taxes and my tax collector was killed. I remarked on it at our last meeting.'

'Yes,' she nodded. 'I remember. You say the youth attacked you. Is he dead?'

'No — not yet.'

'You intend that he shall die?'

He leaned back in his chair. 'Oh I think not. He is a strong youth and should prove useful in the mines or in the brick pits.'

'The girl is his sister, you say she is fair?'

'Yes, unusually so, and has eyes astonishingly blue. She is quite delightful, but . . .' He smiled suddenly though Ashtar glimpsed a wry twist to his lips, 'I took your advice by the way.'

Ashtar bent to retrieve the cup. Her thoughts

raced to the incoherent girl in the sleeping chamber and her heart filled with pity. How her foolishly uttered words had brought pain and horror to another!

'It was quite an experience. Believe me Ashtar, I never thought to meet a maid so ignorant.'

So that was it. Ashtar had heard that desert girls were kept in ignorance of their wifely duties, although it had seemed preposterous to her, brought up in the frank, experienced background of her father's court with its women-folk trained in the worship of Astarte. In this at least, she had been fortunate. She went to Pharaoh's bed unafraid and had found him a skilful and virile lover. She could only dimly guess at the agony of this young slave's experience.

'Well,' she said, forcing her lips to smile, 'at least you can be sure she was a virgin.'

His laugh rang out as he rose. 'That is certainly true. She intrigues me, Ashtar. I terrify her, I'm sure of that, and she is distressed for her brother, yet she will not crawl. Strange that she is unwed. My passion was aroused last night as I have not known it, since my youth, yet I was annoyed by her incompetence. She is no child yet she is immature. She comes from barbarian stock and their women mature late, so I am told. It will be interesting to see how she develops. I must go or I will be late at the Temple.'

Ashtar came back into the sleeping chamber and gazed down at the girl. She sat huddled against the wall, the clothes caught up against her body, fearing the entrance of a stranger.

'So,' she said gently, reaching out to touch the girl's lacerated back, 'you were responsible for Pharaoh's injuries and this was your punishment. Did he do it himself?'

The girl nodded and she sighed and sank down by her side. 'I see.'

Serana caught her hand, 'Thank you for not telling him I was here.'

'You heard?'

'Yes. You think he will spare my brother?'

'He said so. He is not usually cruel and does not needlessly destroy life, though he would be ruthless, if he thought it necessary.'

Serana sank back. All her pain was forgotten now at the thought of Raban. There was hope that he would live and after — who could tell? She watched the other's face. Ashtar had turned away and Serana saw deep sadness in her eyes and distress in the downward curve of her lips. Was this lovely woman in love with Pharaoh? Had what she had heard from him, caused her pain? Above all, Serana wished to spare this woman who had befriended her so readily.

'You love him?' she asked timidly. 'He will tire of me. I can not hope to please him as you can.'

Ashtar's frown vanished and she drew the younger girl into her arms. 'Give your heart peace, little one. I am not jealous. I am distressed that I have caused you harm. I said foolish, thoughtless words to him yesterday and I did not think he would heed them so readily, if at all. Yes I do love him, but not I think as you mean. He favours me and I am content, as you will be, one day.'

The other's face flushed scarlet and Ashtar nodded, 'Yes as you will be — *must* be — in that is your only happiness.'

'I shall never find happiness.'

'Of course you will. I will send my women for food and then we will talk.' She hurried into the other room and gave brisk orders to her attendants, then returned to Serana.

When the attendants entered some minutes later, they brought food and clothing. While they ate Ashtar chattered brightly trying to draw out the girl, so hoping to take her mind from her immediate anxieties. In this she was successful. Serana had never in her short life, managed to find a confidante. The women of her father's household had treated her with respect and envy, while those she had encountered on her journeyings had regarded her generally with suspicion and even hostility. She poured out to this Syrian woman, her love for her father and brother and Ashtar was able to gauge in some part, what her life had been in the Bedouin community that had been her home.

'But all women must become the property of some man,' she said at last. 'Is it so terrible that you now belong to Pharaoh? Is it so different to be given in marriage? What choice would you have had, had your father found a husband for you?' She smiled at the other's evident confusion.

56

So there was a lover, that would explain a great deal.

'I was almost betrothed,' Serana said, turning away her face.

'You were willing?'

She nodded, 'I think so. He was a fine man and I think he would have loved me and treated me kindly. His name was Ischian Ben Ismiel and his father was a wealthy sheik.' She stood up suddenly and went to the garden, staring out over the quiet corner which Ashtar kept free from the chattering magpies in the House of Women. It was indeed very luxurious and lovely. This woman was unquestionably highly favoured. No doubt she had borne Pharaoh several children.

'Do Pharaoh's children have a separate apartment?' she asked. Ashtar was silent before replying and she turned and seeing the expression on the favourite's face, ran impulsively back to her side.

Gently the other took her hand. 'Pharaoh has no children. You have guessed at my sorrow. It grieves me that I have not been able to give him a son.'

'But the other women . . .'

'Yes, it is strange, not one of us able to give him his heart's desire. Can you imagine how honoured will be the woman who bears a child. There was a child, a son, borne of his royal wife and consort, Nefertari. He died when he was almost nine years old, of a plague. Pharaoh's love for the child was such that he concerned himself about no others. The boy was all his joy.'

'And the mother? She is dead?'

'No,' Ashtar hesitated for a moment, 'Pharaoh divorced her. She lives in a house of her own in Memphis.'

'But why, was she unfaithful?'

'In deed I think not, but it is said she loved another. They quarrelled bitterly over the death of the child and in his anger, he put her from him. After the first agony of his sorrow, he found that his fury had gone, but with it, the love he had for her. He has not gone in to her since.' She sighed, 'Poor Nefertari, she loved the life of the court, and now she is doomed for ever to a lonely life, an unwanted and disgraced wife. She will never want for anything, but will never be free.'

'She is free of him,' Serana said softly. 'If I could be so free, I would wish for nothing more.'

'He is a strange, lonely creature,' Ashtar said, quietly, 'you have not known him as I have. He can be cruel and ruthless but there is greatness within his nature. I am not that woman, to unlock that greatness but I pray the gods she may come soon for him and for Egypt.'

Serana looked up at her. The other's face was half turned away but she saw mingled sorrow and tenderness in the set of the lips and sadness in the dark eyes.

'You are very wise,' she said, gently. 'I wish I had your understanding.'

Ashtar laughed, 'You are such a child, Serana.

I am a woman, that is all, and the wisdom of women, *that* I can teach you. We must talk you and I, and then mayhap you will learn from me, the skill that will make your life more tolerable, in the House of Women.'

# 6

Nefren was disturbed. It was difficult to place his finger squarely on the cause of his uneasiness. Pharaoh appeared to be reasonable. He had not had one of his rages in weeks and Pharaoh's moods governed Nefren's peace of mind. Just now, he was planning a visit to his new treasure city in the Delta. The building was progressing well according to the latest reports and he wished to view the site for the new temple.

The women of the harem chattered and quarrelled amongst themselves, discussing the possibility of a favourite being chosen to accompany Pharaoh, but Nefren knew this to be extremely unlikely. On such a project, Pharaoh troubled himself little about women.

The gardens were heavy with scented blossoms. He brushed against stately scarlet lilies and put aside branches of oleander, as he moved on his way.

Ashtar's secluded little garden was a favourite spot. She allowed him free use of it and it was in this direction that he turned his steps. A sudden movement in the bushes arrested his attention. He drew back for a moment into the shadows and waited silently. From Ashtar's room, he saw the pale glow of the oil lamps. A shadow moved across the light, then another. He heard the murmur of voices, one of which he recognised as a man's. Nefren frowned. He knew Ashtar's visitor was not Pharaoh. Could the woman have been foolish enough to invite her lover . . . After a brief moment of indecision, Nefren determined to approach the guilty pair and warn them to be more discreet. He stepped forward, then just as suddenly withdrew again. A man was standing in the garden, his head turned towards Ashtar's apartment. He had his back to Nefren, but appeared to be listening intently.

Silent as a panther and just as deadly in his sudden spring, was Nefren's attack. The other was a powerful man with muscles like iron, but he was completely taken by surprise and could only struggle helplessly in the merciless grip of the slave. Slowly Nefren squeezed tighter and tighter on the other's wind pipe. The intruder writhed and choked in an effort to free himself. The struggle was short and quiet, but Ashtar's ears, sharpened by anxiety, heard the sound and she and Rehoremheb flew to the site of the combat.

'What is it?' she entreated of Nefren in a terrified whisper.

'This spy will not carry tales, I swear it by Set,' Nefren said in a grim whisper.

'Who is he?'

'I do not know. Pharaoh will not wish to know.'

'Wait one moment, Nefren. The man is not an Egyptian.' Her anguished whisper arrested him. He glanced down at the other's apparel then at his face, illuminated by the lamp in Ashtar's apartment, swollen and unrecognisable yet clearly a Semite and not the face of an Egyptian. He loosened his grip on the other's throat. The man's nerveless body slid to the ground while he choked and retched on the grass at their feet.

Rehoremheb gazed fearfully round. 'Bring him into the room for questioning,' he said briefly. 'He must not be found here.'

The two men conveyed the helpless form into Ashtar's room. She closed the shutters, veiling the light and sound from the garden and turned to look down on the stranger.

'He is a desert dweller — a Midianite possibly,' she said briefly. 'See the darkened jowl. He has recently shaved off his beard.'

'Then what is he doing here in the Great House?' Rehoremheb said quickly, 'it is as Nefren says. He is a spy.'

'No I think not — not in the ordinary sense at any rate. Bring me wine.' She shook his arm imperatively and he moved to the table to do her bidding.

Nefren was standing looking down at his prisoner, a puzzled frown darkening his brows. The man was coughing weakly and he put up a questing hand to his injured throat. Rehoremheb returned with the wine and kneeling by his side, Ashtar put the vessel to his lips. His dark eyes moved restlessly from her to the two men then back again to her dusky loveliness.

'Drink and tell us what is your business,' she said quietly.

'The man drank thirstily, coughed again and drew one or two painful breaths. 'I come to find a friend,' he said at last hesitantly, 'I can say no more.' He spoke slowly and his Egyptian was heavily accented.

'A friend?' Rehoremheb's voice was incredulous. 'Do you know where you are?'

The man looked up at him warily. 'This is the palace of Pharaoh?'

'It is,' Nefren said shortly. 'This is the House of Women. Do you not know it is death to enter here?'

'It is perhaps a woman you seek?' Ashtar's voice was very soft. The man made no answer. She turned to the others, 'Leave him with me.' Rehoremheb's face showed consternation and he opened his lips to remonstrate, but she cut him off shortly. 'Please do as I say.' She turned to Nefren. 'See him safely away. He must not be found here and Pharaoh may visit me later.' Nefren looked briefly at the Semite, who was slowly rising to his feet. She shook her head. 'I have nothing to fear. My women are within call if need be. I wish to speak with him. Come back later and bring me news that all is well. 'Go now, my love, with Nefren. The Gods keep you safe.'

Nefren bowed low and walking slightly ahead

of the Egyptian led the way into the garden.

Ashtar listened to their retreating footsteps and then turned back into the room. The intruder was watching her intently. He was better. Colour was beginning to seep back into his waxen countenance and he was breathing more normally.

'You are Ischian Ben Ismiel?'

His eyes widened in astonishment. 'You know me?'

'I guessed that to be your name. Let us say, I know her whom you seek.'

'She is here? My informant was correct then?' His eagerness was pathetic.

She indicated a seat and herself sank down opposite. 'She is a slave in Pharaoh's household.'

He stared at her and she said simply, 'I am sure you are well aware what that position entails.'

He turned away from her and she remained silent. When he at last spoke, the stress of his emotion had emphasised his unfamiliarity with the language, 'Yes, I know,' he said.

'And you still want to help her?'

His eyes gleamed strangely in the lamplight. 'Does she need help? Is she content?'

Ashtar smiled, 'She needs and wants your help now more than ever before, but you must be sensible. You cannot see her now.'

He faced her squarely. 'I will effect her escape if I must kill Pharaoh himself and give my life to do it.'

'Sit down again and listen. I can do little but

advise you. Serana is held in the royal harem. She is closely guarded and she never leaves it except at the express command of Pharaoh.'

'You are the mistress of Pharaoh?'

A slight smile touched her lips. 'I am a lesser wife, shall we say.'

He coloured and bowed his head and she continued. 'The man who attacked you is Pharaoh's personal slave. He may be persuaded to help. If once Serana can be brought from the harem, I will smuggle her from the palace. Ramoses will shortly be leaving on a visit to the Delta. He will not miss one slave girl. When he returns, he will have forgotten her.'

'And it is to your advantage that he will forget her?'

Ashtar's rippling laugh surprised him. 'Do you think the man in my arms was Pharaoh?'

'No,' his confusion showed in the red colour which covered his throat and face, 'but . . . but . . . I . . .'

'But you think I amuse myself with one lover while my lord and master is occupied elsewhere. You are not complimentary, young man. No, I care not who lies in the arms of Pharaoh but I do care that it shall not be little Serana. I have a fondness for her and would give her the happiness she craves if it lies within my power.'

'And you can help us?'

'I can try. Once Serana is out of the palace she must be conveyed to the Hebrew slave village in the Delta. You know it?'

65

'Yes, I know it.'

'Then await her there. Do you know someone there who would receive you and her?'

'I know a stone cutter, Joel. His mother would hide us until we could reach the caravan to Midian.'

'Then go there and wait — twenty days at most, if you have no sign by then, my friend, leave Egypt and at once, for I will have failed. Now you must go. Your presence here is a danger to me as well as to yourself. At any moment Pharaoh may choose to come here. Can you find your way out of the gardens?'

Ischian rose to his feet. 'Yes, lady, I will go for I cannot any longer endanger you. There is no chance of seeing Serana, none at all?'

She shook her head emphatically, 'No, none, until she reaches you at the Hebrew village. Trust me and she will soon be in your arms. Have you some token you can leave her to prove your presence here?'

'There is a chance she may know this waist cloth of mine. I was wearing it on the day we last met.' He unwound it from his waist and thrust it into her hands. It was curiously woven of many colours and a twist of silver thread ran through the weave. Ashtar knew that such articles as this were highly prized among desert men who wore only home dyed cloth except on special occasions. She folded it and placed it upon her table.

'I will see that she receives it. Now go. The blessing of your god go with you.'

He saluted her in eastern fashion, his fingers brushing his heart, head and lips, then he was gone into the night. She strained her ears in the darkness of the garden, but heard only a slight movement in the bushes, then nothing.

Nefren was appalled at her proposal when she outlined the plan to him an hour later. 'Lady, you will destroy us,' he said. 'Assist a woman to escape from Pharaoh's house! Even you would not be safe from his wrath. My fate does not bear contemplation. The whole idea is impossible.'

'No, not impossible if we keep our heads,' she replied, imperturbably. The plan is not so hazardous. You must get the girl out of the women's quarters. I will have Hebrew clothes for her. She will disguise herself. Rehoremheb will convey her on his barge to the Hebrew village, there her lover waits for her. Pharaoh will not even think of her.'

'Will Rehoremheb do this? He will never take part in a risk so deadly.'

She smiled, 'He will do it, never fear.'

'And so easily you say, get her out of the harem. That is the most difficult task of all.'

'There is only one way. Pharaoh must send for her. It is for you and she to see that he notices her. He himself will do the rest. The following morning while he is busy, the girl can be smuggled out of the palace.'

Nefren turned from her, his brain teeming with the temerity of the plan, sounding so easy in a woman's simple reasoning, yet fraught with danger so great that his mind reeled with the horror of it. If they should fail . . . He could not think of that. The girl's face rose up before his eyes, pale and tormented. If she were to stay long in the Great House she would die. He had read these signs before. He turned back to Ashtar. 'I doubt whether I can persuade her, yet I will try.'

Ashtar pressed the waist cloth into his hands. 'Give her this. Tell her it came from her lover and that he will greet her in the Hebrew village, soon, very soon, if only she can be strong.'

# 7

The chatter of the women did not usually interest Serana, but today she had caught snatches of it which arrested her attention. Pharaoh was leaving the city for the Delta. He was to inspect the new buildings and would be gone some time. For a while she would be safe. She shuddered a little and bent over the embroidery she was doing. She sat in her usual position under the tree, slightly withdrawn from the chattering throng by the pool and yet their voices had carried to her even this distance.

At first sight of Nefren she was not alarmed. She looked up as he entered the women's garden and then lowered her eyes to her work. After that first terrible day, the sight of Nefren had filled her with unspeakable terror. Had he not carried her to Pharaoh? His rough kindness had comforted her in her agony and she knew that he wished her well, but the sight of him brought the deadly chill to her body and the uncontrollable shaking of her limbs. Gradually, she grew accustomed to his presence and her fear of him left her. She was not disturbed therefore, when she saw him, but when he came over to the tree where she was sitting, her heart bounded unaccountably and she had to force her trembling hands to stay still on her knee.

'Greetings, lady,' he said quietly, 'it is pleasant here under the tree out of the hot sun.' He glanced back briefly at the women by the pool and then sat beside her on the ground. Her eyes searched his face in mute appeal. Had he bad news of Raban or did he bring her Pharaoh's command? Nefren leaned back outwardly relaxed while his eyes watched the women. Each one hoped he came to bring her Pharaoh's favour but now that they had realised that this was not his intention they paid him no more attention and he was free to talk to Serana undisturbed.

'Lady, I wish to discuss with you matters of grave import but you are not to appear to be listening to anything but idle gossip. Do you understand? No, do not look round. Smile at me and carry on with your work.' He checked her start of sudden alarm, with an encouraging smile. 'Be not alarmed. I bring no bad news.'

She drew an agonised little breath and then smiled back at him. 'I am sorry. Please go on.'

Leaning back, he idly plucked at a lily and began to divest it of its petals. 'Do not start, remember. Do you wish to leave the harem?'

Her eyes closed suddenly and he saw her sway momentarily, then just as quickly she recovered herself. 'You know I would rather die than remain here.'

'There is just a chance. You have friends who

are anxious to help and one who waits for you at the Hebrew village in the Delta. What is your opinion of this weave, lady?'

She started violently as he drew from his robe a broad waist cloth and placed it across her knees. Wonderingly, she touched it. The last time she had glimpsed it, was round Ischian Ben Ismiel's robe as she had stooped to serve him. Had she not then noticed the silver thread admiringly and thought that it must have been a gift from the sheik his father?

'It is very fine,' she said, her voice a little husky.

'It is indeed. It was given to me today by one I met in the market; a desert dweller.' He shook his head as he saw tears well in her lovely eyes. 'Do not weep, lady. Soon you will see him but you must be brave. Your escape depends on you and you alone.'

'What must I do?' Her answer was quick and eager.

He watched her face intently for a moment, then answered brutally, 'You must so charm Pharaoh that he will desire you tonight.'

'Oh no,' her sudden cry was stifled and he saw her fingers tighten on the brightly woven cloth.

'Serana, you must. It is the only way you will leave the harem, only by way of Pharaoh's apartments.'

'I can not do this.'

'I tell you again, it is the only way. Afterwards,' he paused significantly, 'Pharaoh will dismiss you

71

into my care. Then and only then can I help you escape. Tomorrow he leaves for the Delta. He will be busied before he leaves with officials and last minute arrangements. It is then, that you must disappear.'

'I have no skill. How do I charm Pharaoh?' she dropped her eyes while a betraying flush dyed her cheeks. 'I can not even please him. I am ignorant.'

'You must see that he notices you. Later, in the cool of the day, he will come here to give instructions to the attendants and perhaps to choose a woman for the night. It is for you to see he chooses you.'

'But why should he? He has not sent for me since . . . since . . .'

'He has been busy. He may yet find your innocence interesting. Let him see this golden hair of yours.' He pointed to the veil with which in desert fashion, she persisted in hiding her hair. It is quite simple. Speak to him. Drop something in front of him, anything. Surely you are endowed with enough feminine wiles to do this. Well?' His question was bluntly thrown out at her as he rose to his feet.

'I will try,' she said quietly. 'I promise, Nefren. I will try.'

'Choose your loveliest clothes and paint your face. Prepare yourself.' He bowed before her, his eyes betraying the sympathy he felt it unwise to put into words.

She acknowledged his salute with a slight nod

of her head, then once more gave her attention to her work.

Later, inside her sleeping chamber, she gazed long and anxiously at her appearance. Not by any standard, could she be termed beautiful. Her copper mirror showed her the reflection of a pale, haunted face, in which the eyes appeared unusually large, and surrounded by purple shadows. Only her fairness distinguished her from the dark loveliness of her sisters. She had told Nefren the truth. She had no skill to charm the experienced palate of Pharaoh. Only in her innocence was she any different from all the other women. She did not want Pharaoh's attentions. In that alone was she separate and in that alone would she have any chance of catching his notice.

She dressed in her simplest robe of white, let down the shimmering mass of her hair and taking the khol stick drew only the lightest of lines round her large eyes. This would emphasise her fear. She was afraid, that would be no act, and yet it might serve her purpose. She gave one quick glance at her appearance and sat down within her chamber to wait. For the only time since she had come to Egypt Serana prayed — she knew not to whom, 'Let him notice me, make me desirable in his eyes, so may I achieve my release from this hell.'

The attendants ordered all the women into the central garden. Serana drew back into the shadows of her chamber and waited. When the eager chattering of the woman stopped, she knew Pharaoh

73

had entered the garden. She heard his voice, resonant and demanding, as he instructed the chief eunuch, then his amused laugh as he spoke to one or another of the women.

It was then that Serana moved in the shadows. Fer-nut, the chief attendant, turned and saw her white garment outlined against the doorway and called to her in a shrill voice.

Serana drew back, her heart beating so fast that it threatened to break from her breast. The woman entered the room her dark eyes flashing angrily at the disobedience of the slave girl.

'Did you not hear the order? All of you are to go out. You are not properly attired. How dare you disobey.'

Pharaoh's voice came to her half amused, as she remembered it. 'Let me see the woman who hides her face from me. Bring her out, Fer-nut.'

Serana was dragged into the garden. She resisted Fer-nut's angry jerks, and fell forward at last before the feet of Pharaoh.

'So,' he bent down and lifted her face, his black eyes flashing with amusement. 'It is our little desert maiden. See, Nefren, how she hates me, when so many fawn on me. It will be interesting to see if I can change her ideas.' He released her abruptly and turned to Fer-nut, 'See that she is brought to me tonight. Come, Nefren, there is still much to be done.' He turned swiftly and strode away from the women's quarters.

She stood a little dazed, watching him as he strode off. Behind her, she heard the excited twit-

74

tering of the women. They surrounded her, complimenting her on her good fortune and commenting on her appearance. Pushing her way free of them, she ran into her chamber and throwing herself on the bed, she wept bitterly.

When Fer-nut came for her, she stifled her rising panic and went submissively. The two attendants spent an hour lovingly preparing her for the arms of Ramoses. They rubbed sweet smelling oils into her body and even into the roots of her hair. When she moved, a heavy sweet fragrance floated from her. The two girls chattered incessantly. Serana strove to ignore their advice and fulsome compliments. They painted her eyes and attired her in linen so fine it was almost transparent. At last she was ready and when Nefren came to convey her to Pharaoh's apartments, she saw his approval in his eyes and knew she was lovely.

He took her cold little hand and drew her through the passages. 'Have courage, little one. It will be soon over and you will be free.'

She gave one convulsive little squeeze to his hand as he gently released her and she passed into the private apartment of her royal master.

He was standing by the great open window and he turned as she entered and his eyes ran over her slim form and up to the golden crown of hair falling on to her shoulders. A smile curved the corners of his lips.

'So my little innocent has arrived. Tell me again. What is your name?'

'It is Serana, lord.' Her answer was half whispered.

'Ah yes, I remember. Your brother attempted to kill me.' He laughed again at the alarm in her face. 'Do not fear. He lives still. My overseer tells me he is a good worker.'

'Your gods will reward you for your mercy,' she said fervently and his fierce black eyes softened for a moment.

'They have given me you,' he said quietly and he ran gentle fingers up her arm. Instinctively, she drew away and he laughed again. 'Still so ignorant and virginal? Come, my child, why did Ptah fashion you so finely, do you think, were it not to give pleasure to men?'

Angrily she retorted, her blue eyes for once blazing with unconcealed fury, 'If there be gods, I can not believe that they made women as playthings for any man, king or otherwise.'

'But women are made to bear children to their husbands.'

'Children yes, and to be devoted wives waiting on their husband's needs, and listening to his ideals and worries, true and loyal partners.'

'What strange ideas you have in your Bedouin tents. So you think I would discuss matters of state with my wives?'

'You could, if you chose wisely, lord.'

'I want no advice or counsel from you, little one. Ashtar tells me she has instructed you well. I am interested in your progress.'

Fear turned Serana cold. She fought back the

deadly chill and feeling of sickness as he lifted her in his arms. She did not resist. It was quite useless and she knew it.

This must be endured and for Raban's sake, she would not antagonise this man. When his lips pressed lingeringly on her shoulder and throat she made no withdrawal and lay passive in his arms.

When the first light of morning flooded the chamber, Serana gazed down at the sleeping man by her side. His strong hard body was relaxed and at peace. The unusual sensitive mouth smiled and the whole face appeared childlike and satisfied. She moved slightly and he let her slide from his arms, without restraint. All night she had stayed wakeful while he slept by her side.

The experience had not been so devastating as that first night. Ashtar's worldly wise advice had prepared her and she had steeled herself against resistance. She knew the man by her side to be a gentle and skilful lover, yet the thought of remaining his property filled her with sick horror. She knew now that she must escape. Death would be preferable to this unthinkable bondage.

He woke suddenly and put out an arm in search of her. She allowed him to sleepily caress her body.

'Little Serana, are my arms so distasteful? I think you have learned well, so well I am half a mind to take you with me to the Delta.'

She stiffened in his arms and caught back an

imperceptible cry of horror.

'But no, I think not. When I return you will be even more lovely and I think not altogether displeased to see me, though I fear you will not confess it.'

Once awake the boundless energy had returned. He stood up and sounded the gong by the bedside.

'Arise my love. Nefren will take you back to the harem. I will send you a necklace to bring out the beauty of your eyes. Perhaps faience, it is a delicate blue and lovely, though possibly not to your taste as much as lapis or sapphires. We shall see. My favours can do much for you.'

Nefren answered the summons. Serana saw his eyes move restlessly over the room attempting to gauge the situation.

'You will convey this little one to the women's quarters. Tell them I am pleased with her and she is to be treated well. If she wishes she can be escorted into the city to buy whatever her heart desires. The goods will be paid for. Good-bye, my love, your loveliness will haunt me until I return. Grow yet more beautiful for me.' He kissed her hands and tilted her chin so that she was forced to look full into his dark eyes.

'Grant me one smile and a kiss of your own free will.' Serana felt repugnance for the trick she had played on him sweep through her. She closed her eyes, then rising on tiptoe, kissed him full on the mouth and smiled.

'I will try to be a good plaything,' she said

though the lie scorched her lips.

He put her from him and stood, hands on hips, regarding her. 'You see, Nefren, the wildcat is half tamed — not completely yet but she will be. Take her from me quickly or I will not wish to part with her and there is a great deal to do.'

Her last sight of him, as Nefren hurried her from the room, was one she would always carry in her heart. He had turned his attention to a roll of papyrus on a table. He had already forgotten her and was engrossed in the plans for the Delta city.

# 8

Nefren bundled Serana into a small room near to Pharaoh's suite.

'Here you will find a bundle of clothes such as those worn by the Hebrew slave women. Ashtar purchased these for you in the market. You are to change quickly, rub some of that dark salve into your skin and most important of all, cover that golden hair. Keep it well out of sight. I must return to Pharaoh and assist him to bathe and attire him for the day. I shall be gone some time. Do not be afraid, no one comes near this room.'

In a flash he had left her and she turned her attention to the clothes on the bed. They were of home-spun wool, a gown in dark blue and a head veil of white. The rough wool felt homely to the touch and she braided up her fair hair, quickly pushing it well under the concealing head-cloth then sat down on the bed and waited. The least noise in the corridor outside filled her with trepidation. She had promised Nefren she would not stir from the room and she intended to keep that oath. It seemed an interminable time while she sat and stared at the bare ceiling.

A scratching at the door brought her to her

feet suddenly one hand on her heart. She stood still making no sound.

A feminine voice called softly, 'Nefren.' There was a pause and then it came again, 'Nefren are you within?' As there was no answer, Serana prayed that whoever it was, would conclude that the room was empty and go away. She waited in an agony of suspense, then the door opened slowly and a woman advanced quickly into the room. With a glad little cry Serana flung herself into the outstretched arms of Ashtar.

The older woman divested herself of the concealing veils she had worn and drew Serana to herself. On Ashtar's bosom the pent-up emotion broke at last into a storm of weeping. Gently Ashtar stroked the bowed head and when at last it subsided, tilted up the tear stained face and gazed at her long and hard.

'This weeping must cease, little Serana, for there is much to be done. You have played your part well, now we must play ours. In a few moments Nefren will take you to the landing stage and you must be quite ready to go with him.'

'I am to escape by boat?'

'Yes, listen carefully. Pharaoh goes to the new treasure city today in the royal barge. With him in his own boat, goes Rehoremheb, the master builder. He will convey you safely to your lover in the Delta. Trust him and obey him implicitly.'

'But this is terribly dangerous. I am to travel in Pharaoh's own party. Oh Ashtar, we will be discovered and . . .'

'Now why should you fear, foolish one? Pull yourself together. The two men will not meet on the journey, or if they do, Rehoremheb will be summoned to the royal barge. You will not be seen.'

'But the risk to him!'

'I have considered the risk to him.' Ashtar's voice was low, and Serana turned and stared at her suddenly.

'Then . . .'

'The life of my love is in your hands, Serana. The gods know how I love you to trust him to you. You will be circumspect and not fail me. One little mistake . . .'

'Dear, dear, Ashtar,' Serana covered the concubine's hands with ardent kisses, 'I will not fail you. I promise he will come back to you.'

Ashtar smiled through the veil of sudden tears which had sprung to her eyes. 'Then the gods go with you both. May they deliver you safely to your lover.'

When Nefren hurried into the room, even his usually impassive features showed traces of strain. His cursory glance took in the transformation in Serana's appearance and he nodded in relief. 'The disguise is good. It should serve us well. First this,' he held out an elaborate necklace of heavy gold studded with turquoise, curiously chased and wrought, a masterpiece of the goldsmith's art. Serana took it wonderingly.

'For me?' her eyes opened in amazement. Never had she held anything so valuable or lovely.

'For you — a mark of Pharaoh's approbation.' His answer was dry. 'It seems you played your part consuminately.'

'But I can't take it.'

'Why not, it is yours.'

'No, I can't, you know I can't. She pushed it back at him, her face colouring under the tan. 'It is not mine by right. I . . . I don't want it.'

Nefren took the necklace and roughly pushed it back into her hand. 'You will take it. It may serve you well, who knows?'

Ashtar nodded, 'Nefren is right Serana, Ramoses will never miss it. To him it is a trumpery thing — a sign of his approval. To you, it might mean your life. It would be foolishness to refuse it.'

Nefren turned to Ashtar briskly, 'All is ready lady, we must go. Pharaoh is consulting with his vizier and will be closeted with him for an hour. Rehoremheb waits at the landing stage. Serana must go aboard at once.'

Ashtar kissed Serana gently. She gave the girl a little push towards Nefren and tried not to look disturbed as the two went from her. She waited for a few moments to regain her composure before making her way back to her own apartments. Pharaoh would doubtless visit her before taking his departure and for him she must be beautiful.

Nefren hurried Serana through the palace gardens and into the city. At every moment she dreaded instant discovery. The palace itself and the courtyards were crowded with people but they were all so busy that they did not so much as glance in their direction. Charioteers, guards, boatmen, court officials, shaven-headed priests, all were gathered to see Pharaoh leave for the Delta. Many were to accompany him on his journey. She also was to accompany him. A cold feeling of fear touched her heart at the thought, but Nefren relentlessly hurried her on.

The landing place was also packed with people. The townsfolk were in holiday mood, clad in their best, gossiping and singing, while they waited to catch a glimpse of the Divine Son of Ra as he stepped on to the royal barge. Many carried flowers to strew before him. Four great barges were secured to the landing stage. Serana took the scene in quickly as she was hurried down the broad white steps to the third of the ships in the line. It was a light craft though large enough. The steersman took her by the hand and drew her aboard as he recognised Nefren. Serana found herself led below to where the master sat in the small cabin surrounded by rolls and rolls of papyrus. He rose to his feet, bowing slightly and his voice was pleasing and musical. Even at that first meeting, Serana knew why Ashtar loved this man so dearly.

'Welcome aboard. It was well timed. We have just time to show you to your quarters and to make you comfortable before I must go to see Pharaoh embark, then to see to our sailing.'

Nefren took both her hands and raised them

to his lips. 'The gods be good to you, lady. If they are kind, you will soon be safe in your own land.'

Serana's eyes were wet with tears at this parting. She could hardly speak her thanks. 'The gods deal well with you too, Nefren, as you have dealt with me. I can not tell you how great I realise is the risk you run for me, nor how I will pray for you for ever, for your part in it.'

He smiled at her, that strange half sad smile, then bowing to the master builder, he left the cabin. She heard the patter of his sandals on deck and his muffled remark to one of the crew then he was gone.

Rehoremheb smiled, 'He must go, if Pharaoh misses him there will be questions asked in the palace, now let me show you your quarters.'

A tiny cabin had been prepared aft. Serana noticed how cleanly it had been swept and a mattress and blankets had been prepared for her. The place was airy and secluded. She thanked Rehoremheb gravely.

'You will not need to stay here all the time. Once we sail, there is no reason why you should not venture on deck.' His smiling mouth parted showing a gleam of white teeth. 'If a woman is seen veiled on my barge it will not excite comment but for the rest of the day it is imperative that you stay well hidden. There may be a hue and cry in the House of Women.'

'I understand and will obey.'

'Good.' He smiled down at her. I go now to

the landing stage, sleep well.' He turned back for a moment. If you stand in the shadow of the cabin, you will see the pageantry. It is a rare sight.'

Serana turned back to the cabin that was to shelter her until they reached the Delta. She sank down for a moment on to the bed. She felt flushed and tired. She had had no sleep the previous night and for a few blessed moments it was bliss to sink back in utter privacy and let her tired body rest. Above her she could hear the men moving about, preparing to cast off, when the master returned. They called to one another and one was singing. From the landing stage the sound of an excited crowd reached her. The noise swelled louder. Pharaoh was approaching. Shouts of acclamation greeted him.

Serana sprang to her feet and drew her veiling over her face. She must see him once more, in all his glory. She stepped to the cabin door, and standing in its shadow as Rehoremheb had directed, looked across at the royal landing stage, where the crowd was thickest. The great barge stood waiting, its silken sails shining in the sun, its carved prow gaily painted. An awning had been erected to shield Pharaoh from the fierce heat of the sun for he would stay in full view of his people while the boat made its slow progress down river to the Delta.

The chanting of the priests began. They were blessing the enterprise, praying that the new city would rise triumphantly above the flat wastes of the Delta. They prayed that the gods would keep their own son in safety during the journey. Serana saw him then, standing proud and unsmiling on the quay. He was wearing a tunic of white linen and a heavily embroidered cloak reaching to his sandals. The sun caught the golden bracelets and jewels he was wearing and made them scintillate in the golden light. Today he was not wearing the crown of the Two Lands but a striped headdress surmounted by the golden uraeus. The crowd was stilled suddenly as he addressed them. Serana was too far away to hear what was said. Again the populace acclaimed him, then regally he mounted the barge followed by the priests and the members of the household who were to accompany him.

Serana withdrew into the cabin and sat down again. In a few moments the noise above her grew louder. Rehoremheb was coming aboard. The anchor was raised and the barge embarked. Serana lay on her mattress listening. Soon they would be miles away from the House of Women, but its master sat in the barge ahead barely a few yards from her.

# 9

As the barge made its slow leisurely way down river, one day Serana heard Rehoremheb call her eagerly. She emerged from her cabin, to find him laughing and slightly winded. The royal party had drawn up close to a small Nile village and he had been ashore with Pharaoh and others of the royal household. There had been some talk of wildfowling early the next morning.

'Serana, little Serana,' he laughed, 'at last, some real action.'

'What is it? You are quite flushed with excitement.'

'And so I should. We go to hunt a lion.'

'A lion,' Serana's cheeks paled.

'Yes, we borrow two light chariots. It seems it has been terrorising the village. Two children have been killed and Pharaoh proposes a hunt. The animal is probably wounded otherwise it would never come so near the village.'

'Rehoremheb, take care, for Ashtar's sake.'

'Don't worry, little Serana. I shall take care for my own sake. It is some time since I went on a hunt, but my hand has not yet lost its cunning.' He weighed three spears carefully, balancing them in his hand to his satisfaction, and nodded. 'Good, these will do well.' He was all boyish impatience and eagerness for the chase and throwing a warning to keep herself secluded, he hurried out of the cabin.

She heard him answer similar impatient calls from the landing stage, then came the jingle of harness, the sounds of weapons and whips. Above them all, she heard the voice of Pharaoh calling to his companions and then they were off. Not until the sounds had died away in the distance, did she come on deck. Along where the line of desert stretched away from the mud walled little houses, she saw the tell tale dust rise where Pharaoh's line of chariots had caused a small sand storm behind them.

She busied herself with minor tasks and then settled herself under the awning on deck as the day's heat became intense. The sailors dozed. The sun beat pitilessly on the little village, and half asleep herself, she wondered how the men could be so energetic. Not expecting them to return until much later, she was jolted suddenly awake, at the sound of horses' hoofs coming close and stood up, fearfully at the call of the man who boarded the barge. It was Nefren.

'Lady,' he came to an abrupt halt as she emerged pale and trembling from the cabin.

'What is it, Nefren? What is wrong? Pharaoh is injured?'

'Pharaoh? No, Rehoremheb.' He was poised to throw his spear when his chariot overturned and he fell at the feet of the beast. It sprang of course. Only the prompt intervention of Pharaoh saved his life, but I fear he is badly mauled and may yet die.'

'No, oh no, Nefren, tell me quickly what happened? How did Pharaoh save him?'

'We tracked the beast by his spoor. We were right, it was a male lion badly wounded in the right fore-foot. This was obviously why it attacked the people of the village. Rehoremheb was way ahead in his chariot and prepared to attack when he was thrown. His charioteer had driven too carelessly. The fool was thrown clear, but lay where he fell too witless to assist Rehoremheb. Our chariot drew into sight and we heard the savage noise of the beast. Man and animal were so closely intertwined that it was impossible for Pharaoh to throw his spear without fear of transfixing Rehoremheb. He hurled himself out of the chariot and on foot got himself into a better position for the throw. He caught the huge beast squarely in the throat, but it was a near thing.'

'No one else is injured?'

'No — only Rehoremheb's charioteer, the helpless fool, who seems to have a sprained foot. I must go now to the royal barge and summon Ptah Hoten. He is a healer priest, thank the Gods he travels with us.'

'Nefren, wait, what are they doing with Rehoremheb?'

'They will bring him here to his own barge which will be more comfortable and cleaner than the village. When I left they had made a rude litter from the broken chariot and were carrying him more slowly. It will be some time before they get back. They must travel with care.'

'The healer — he will save him?'

Nefren shook his head 'I know not, Ptah Hoten is high priest of the Temple. He is a skilled surgeon. If he cannot save him, no one can. I must inform him so he is prepared to receive the sick man.' He made to leave then swiftly turned, his eyes suddenly hard, 'You must be prepared, anything might happen. Pharaoh himself may board the barge.'

She heard him calling to the men to inform them of the emergency. She stood for a few moments dazed, too alarmed at the tragedy that had struck at the gay, laughter-loving builder to be aware of her own plight. So shocked was she, that she had not taken refuge in her cabin, and was still on deck when Ptah Hoten, the High Priest, arrived to prepare for his patient.

There was something in his serene, unhurried gait and fine countenance that calmed her fears and in spite of herself, she found herself bowing her head before the gaze of his steady grey eyes. He was accompanied by a young temple server, bearing his instruments. The priest's voice was low and pleasant, calm and unhurried like his bearing.

'Child, you know that Rehoremheb is wounded.'

She inclined her head.

'We shall require a low table, scrubbed perfectly clean. You know of one?'

She led him to the cabin and pointed to Rehoremheb's work bench, strewn with plans and rolls of blank papyrus. The young server cleared it and drew it towards the light. The priest placed a wooden box on a stool and drew from it, a collection of bronze implements, several small alabaster pots, presumably containing salves and ointments and a small phial of dark liquid. 'Can you find me a plentiful supply of linen, and wine to cleanse the wound?'

She nodded and entering the part of the cabin curtained off for Rehoremheb's sleeping chamber, found two tunics of fine unbleached linen and tearing them into long strips returned to his side. He thanked her quietly and dispatched the slave to bid the sailors prepare a fire on shore and heat a plentiful supply of water.

'And now, my child,' he said quietly subsiding on to a stool, 'we must wait, sit down and reserve your strength.'

She inclined her head and sat down as he bade her, drawing her head veil close to conceal the greater part of her features. She noticed how controlled was his body. He sat in perfect repose, his hands lightly resting on his knees. A lesser man would have fidgeted, impatient for a sight of his patient. This man waited quietly. Instinctively Serana felt the power flow from his relaxed figure into her own. In his presence she could have no fear. She was content to leave the fate of Rehoremheb in those beautiful hands. She watched him as he sat withdrawn, his face towards the village, his mind abstracted. The light fell on his fine serious features, the beauty of which was heightened by the severity of his shaven head.

'You love Rehoremheb?' his question seemed not impertinent, he really wished to know. She did not prevaricate.

'No, priest, but I am very fond of him.'

'Nevertheless you are his woman?'

'He is my protector but he is taking me to my own people in the Hebrew village.'

He inclined his head satisfied and was silent again.

Rehoremheb looked already a corpse when they bore him carefully into the cabin. His face was leaden, his lips bloodless and he breathed stertorously. Serana was shocked by the suddenness of the change in him. Ptah Hoten took control, indicating silently where he wished the wounded man to be placed and bent his head over his patient. The bearers left, whispering anxiously. Serana drew back into the shadows as Pharaoh strode imperiously into the cabin.

'How bad is it?' he said, anxiety deepening the harshness of his tone.

The other's answer was controlled, 'He is badly mauled, there will be poison in the wounds and fever may set in. If there is resistance to infection he will live.'

'You will stay with him?'

'Yes, lord.'

For the first time Serana detected a note of uncertainty in Pharaoh's voice. 'Is there anything I can do?'

A faint smile curled the lips of the priest. 'No, lord, there is nothing, do not be troubled, you have done your part, or he would not now be here.'

Ramoses shrugged. 'I like the lad,' his voice trailed off, 'he is useful to me.' Still the other's smile did not alter.

'He will live, Ptah Hoten?'

'By the mercy of the Gods, yes.'

Ramoses relaxed. 'Then I will leave you to your task unhindered by my useless presence. 'By the way,' he swung round on his heel abruptly, 'if he talks nonsense in his fever do not heed it. He is lovesick, in love with love itself.' His fierce eyes had glimpsed Serana and he beckoned her forward impatiently. 'You are his woman?'

Stricken with terror, Serana could do nothing but nod and attempt to hide her features by pulling her head veil forward. But he was not really concerned for her but the sick man. His eyes softened and he touched her shoulder in a comforting grip.

'Do not fear. Ptah Hoten is a great healer. He will save him.' Then without another glance at the almost fainting girl, he swept from the cabin.

Ptah Hoten's gaze took in her ashen face, but he said nothing, indicating that he wished to begin work. Without need for instruction she fetched water and watched him. He cleansed the terrible wounds, pouring in a quantity of spirit to burn out any poison left by the claws of the beast, then once more, he washed the wound and smoothed on healing salve. Serana was amazed at the skill of those fingers, which drew together the gaping sides of the gashes so they would heal cleanly without scars, under the linen bandages. He laid a hand on the forehead of the sick man, noting with a little shake of the head the heavy drops of sweat which stood out on his brow, then he inclined his ear to listen to the heart-beat.

'I fear there will be fever, but he has a strong constitution and should survive complications. Fortunately, there is no internal damage.'

'Will he live, priest?'

'I think so, but only the gods hold the fate of man. Pray for him.'

'The god of my fathers no longer hears my prayers, oh priest,' Serana said, bitterly.

'Then, child, pray to his and they may hear.'

Rehoremheb spent a restless night. He tossed and turned, thrusting off the soft blankets in his fever. Sweat stood out on his forehead and in his delirium he called out to Ashtar, words spilling from him unheeded. Serana was terrified for him. Her eyes sought those of the priest, but he seemed completely unmoved by these disclosures, every now and then stooping to wipe the sweat streaked brow and to replace the covering.

'Do not despair,' he said quietly, 'the fever will break in the morning. I will give him a cooling draught and it is possible that he may sleep then.'

He turned to his equipment and taking a cup of water, poured into it, some of the dark liquid from the phial. 'Lift his head a little, can you, and I will try to get him to swallow some of this.'

Half an hour later, Rehoremheb fell into an uneasy doze. By morning the fever had broken and when Serana gazed down at him in the first light, he had curled up like a child asleep. Already the comeliness of his countenance had returned and she knew, with a swift stab of relief, that he would recover. Her eyes met those of the healer priest across the bed.

'Thank you, priest.'

'Pharaoh deserves more praise than I, for it was his spear that delivered our young friend, for the rest, he is strong enough now to allow the wounds to heal well and cleanly. His beauty will not be marred. The ladies will be relieved on that score.'

By the afternoon of the following day Rehoremheb was sitting up and taking food. He talked boastfully and charmingly of the hunt and his gratitude to Pharaoh, Ptah Hoten he treated with great deference and ceased his gay badinage when the priest was near. Ptah Hoten declared him so far recovered that it was no longer necessary for him to stay in attendance and returned to the royal barge, giving instructions to Serana as to his care. She watched him disembark and then returned to Rehoremheb who called her imperatively to his side.

'Little Serana, I thank you for helping to care for me.' She smiled, then taking her hand, he looked anxiously into her eyes. 'The High Priest, did he hear anything he should not? Did I talk foolishly in my delirium?'

Serana avoided his eyes and he pulled at her hand, forcing her to look at him. 'He did?'

'I think,' she said at last, 'you have nothing to fear from Ptah Hoten. He is a very holy man.'

He sank back against the cushions. 'We must wait then and see. It is Ashtar who concerns me. The gods grant that she remains safe.'

Serana hesitated and then said very softly and slowly, 'I think that Pharaoh knows.'

His head jerked up abruptly. 'You think what!'

'I think that he knows — about you and Ashtar. He told Ptah Hoten not to heed your ravings. He himself was doubtful about leaving you.'

'It is impossible.'

'No, I think not. He loves Ashtar, truly loves her, he is not in love with her. There is a difference. You must not be jealous, Rehoremheb, for the loveliest and greatest woman in all Egypt loves you with all of her heart, but you must yourself take care, or you will destroy her.'

He nodded. 'If it is true what you say, then he did a great thing indeed when he saved my life.'

'He took a double risk, his own life and that of his concubine's, for every moment you exist she is in danger.'

'I must be more circumspect,' he muttered

wincing suddenly with pain, as he moved care-lessly, 'or my love will feed the sacred crocodiles of the Temple of Ammon and I . . .' he gave a short harsh laugh, 'but we will not think of that. Little Serana, you will soon be in your lover's arms. One more day's sailing and we will reach the Hebrew village. Then you will be free. Think of me a little, when you sit with your children round you, in your own tents.'

She flushed and bending, kissed his handsome forehead lightly. 'I will think of you often, dear Rehoremheb, and of Ashtar and Nefren.'

'And of Pharaoh?' he lifted one eyebrow, quiz-zically.

'And of Pharaoh,' she said, as she rose to her feet.

# 10

The third day from the hunt, Rehoremheb was better. He again ate and drank with relish and no longer winced or went white to the lips with pain at the least movement. Within two days he would be on his feet again and the great barges resume their journey to the Delta.

Her first sight of the new treasure city was unforgettable. The barges were tethered to the landing stage which was a hubbub of activity. Ahead of them, lay a huge ship bearing enormous slabs of limestone for building. For the first time Serana saw a long line of slaves heaving at the ropes, pulling the great slabs up the ramps towards the building site. Pity welled up in her heart as she watched the pathetic train, pulling, straining, directed by the taskmasters who organised them. Rehoremheb came behind her and touched her arm lightly.

'It is not as you think. They do not harm themselves. The work is hard, but they do only short shifts.' He laughed boyishly, 'I know, I arranged it. The blocks come from the quarries up river. We build a temple to Ptah and it is for this reason that Ptah Hoten travels with us. They are not starved, they could not do the work well if they were and the lash is always necessary. These men are slaves. They will not pull together unless they are made to.'

'They are treated like animals. Have you no pity?'

His eyes widened in astonishment. 'How strangely you talk. Of course I have pity. I tell you the slaves are treated well, as far as I can ensure it.'

'But you are not always here and taskmasters are often cruel.'

'True,' he nodded, 'I have had to deal firmly with one or two, but the majority are sensible men. See — the shift is over, the block is up the ramp. Watch now, the men will let go the harness ropes and return to their women in the village. For three hours the heat will be unbearable and no work can be done. Come under the awning and stop distressing yourself. You cannot free all the slaves in the world and would not if you could.'

'I have been a slave, Rehoremheb. I know what it feels to be caged,' she turned away from the sight and did as he bade her, stooping to enter the cabin.

'Come you are not angry with me, little Serana,' he coaxed patting the stool by his side, his fine eyes laughing at her.

'It is impossible to be angry with you for long. You are like a child. Forgive me, Rehoremheb, I shall ever be grateful to you — but I think of Raban all the time, I think and remember.'

'Your brother? I will enquire about him. If I can, I will take him into my service. There, will that satisfy you?'

She jumped up eagerly. 'You will do this — may your gods bless you, Rehoremheb.'

'Now we must think of you. Soon Pharaoh will visit the site of the new temple. I have persuaded Ptah Hoten that I am fit enough to accompany them. I shall ensure that the party is fully occupied for some hours. During that time, Nefren will take you to your lover in the village. Now come and eat for the last time of the fleshpots of Egypt. Nowhere in your Bedouin tents will you get food so fine.'

She tossed her head and made to give a sharp answer then suddenly laughed and sank down by his side. It was impossible to take offence at Rehoremheb's teasing.

The sun stood high in the heavens when Nefren boarded the barge and told her quietly he was ready. Already the royal party had left for the building site and she could hear Rehoremheb's voice explaining his arrangements as they went. The royal answer she did not catch.

'Is it safe?' she said.

'Quite safe. Come Ischian waits for you and wishes to leave tonight.'

For one moment she regretted leaving the barge without one more glimpse of her host. His companionship had become dear to her. She would always remember him with affection. Then her thoughts returned to Ischian who waited for her and she veiled herself quickly and followed her guide without a word.

The Hebrew village consisted of a cluster of small mud-daubed huts some way from the building site. In the centre was a well and as they approached, a woman drew a pitcher of water and turned to face them. Nefren spoke to her briefly in passing and led Serana to the end hut. He stopped, motioned her to stand behind him and knocked. The door was opened by an old man who glanced at Serana and gestured them quickly to come inside.

The interior of the hut was dark and it took some moments for Serana to accommodate herself to her surroundings. A man came forward from the shadows. He held out his arms and in a second Serana was sobbing against his chest.

Ischian stroked her hair silently. He said nothing. When it was over he pulled her gently to a stool and made her sit. Her legs were trembling and she was glad of a moment's respite while he moved away to pour water into a bowl for her. She kept her eyes down while she drank. She did not want to look at Ischian. Now all at once she felt unclean and dreaded to meet his gaze.

Nefren spoke softly and Ischian went over to him. They conversed for a moment in whispers then he called over to her.

'I must leave you now, lady, the Gods guard you.'

'Dear Nefren I can never truly thank you — but I will remember you always.'

He kissed her hands then looked steadily into her eyes. For a moment she could not gauge his expression then abruptly he touched her cheek — bowed in eastern fashion to Ischian and moved hurriedly out of the hut. An unaccountable feeling of loss smote her and she almost called him back but choking back the cry she turned and with shaking fingers attempted to put to rights her appearance and at last faced Ischian.

He shook his head gently.

'Do not be afraid, Serana. You need say nothing.'

'You know?' Her eyes mutely asked the question.

He nodded quietly. 'All I wish to know. It is enough that you are safe. Now you must try to forget.'

'I wish to go with you to your tents — let me serve you, Ischian.'

'You will go with me as my betrothed wife as I always considered you.'

'But I — Your father he will think . . .'

'It matters not what anyone thinks if I wish it — and I do, simply trust me and do as I say.'

She nodded, too full to speak, and placed her hand in his.

An hour after the sun had vanished abruptly below the horizon, Ischian drew the heavily veiled Serana out of the slave village. They walked quickly and she shivered a little now that she was bereft of the sun's scorching rays. Ischian knew his way and guided her surely and silently. She gave a little sob when she saw the familiar caravan with its group of kneeling camels and welcoming fires.

'Hush now, you must be brave.' Ischian said gently. 'You must think no more of your father.'

'But Raban, I leave him to suffer.'

'Raban loved you far too much to wish you to stay penned when you could be free. Now go and rest. There is a tent prepared for you. We start early in the morning.'

When Serana awoke the following morning she was violently and unaccountably sick. Bewildered and wretchedly weak, she lay for a while in the tent, and Ischian gently ordered her to rest.

'It is the reaction. You are tired and worried. Rest for an hour, then we will start. A short delay will do no harm.'

'It must be something I ate. I am never sick.'

'We are all sick at times. I think you were afraid of meeting me. You have been under a terrible strain. The effect is distressing but you'll soon get over it.'

He nodded reassuringly, and left the tent. Serana lay still, staring at the flap opposite. When she rose a few moments later, she was once more sick and sank back on the sleeping mat, over-come with weakness and hot tears of misery.

When Ischian returned to tell her they were ready to begin, the bout had left her. He noted the pallor of her complexion and the deep violet shadows under her eyes, but he passed no comment. The slight breeze of early morning refreshed her and she soon recovered her spirits. After the luxury of the House of Women she found the heat of the desert sand, which cut her skin and tortured her with thirst, unduly wearying and was glad to rest when they camped for the night. Her sickness of the early morning had apparently left her over fatigued and Ischian found her unusually silent over the meal.

The next day she was once more sick and the day after, and soon Serana could no longer hide from herself the truth she was afraid to face. She was with child. She had no experience to guide her, but womanly intuition pointed the facts. The signs were unmistakable. The first day she forced herself to accept the truth, she crept away from the evening camp and hiding behind a rock, she threw herself on the ground and gave way to quiet but desperate weeping. It was here that Ischian discovered her.

As gentle as any woman he stroked her hair and tried to comfort her.

Savagely, she pushed him from her but he persisted and at last she looked at him and threw back her straggling hair which had escaped from its confining head veil. 'Leave me, Ischian, there is no comfort you can give me. I am to have a child.'

His face remained grave but unmoved. 'I guessed it.'

She stared at him wonderingly. 'You knew?'

'I was not sure. It seemed likely.'

'And you are not angry?'

'Why should I be angry? I am distressed for you of course.'

'But this is Pharaoh's child. Oh Ischian, what am I to do . . . what can I do?'

'This changes nothing.'

'It changes everything Ischian. How can I return with you now? It is impossible.'

He drew her firmly to her feet. 'Nothing is impossible. Of course you will return with me. You are my betrothed wife. So you will soon have a child. There will be talk but that we can ignore. It will not be pleasant but it will pass.'

'You say it changes nothing, Ischian, but there is the child to be thought of.'

'I had not forgotten that. It will not be easy to accept the child, knowing what I do — but he will be yours. When he is born you must decide. If you wish to keep him, then I shall be content. If not, we must find some childless couple who will be prepared to care for him.'

'You love me enough to keep another man's child in your tents?'

He didn't answer for a moment and then he said directly, 'Did you love the father?'

'No.' Her answer was immediate, just as direct, then a flush dyed her cheeks and she avoided his eyes, 'But I . . . can't explain . . . I . . .'

'Don't hate him,' he finished it for her and she inclined her head.

'I feared him terribly.' She shuddered and sat

down again on the sand with her back to him and lifting a handful of the powdery grains, let them sift from her fingers. 'The first time he . . .' she broke off and swallowed, 'I can't talk about it . . . but I must be frank and honest, there was another time which need never have been. He would not have noticed me again but I made him . . . I wanted to get free from the House of Women and they told me it was the only way.'

'And this time was different,' he prompted her softly.

She nodded and stood up just as abruptly. He realised with sudden clarity that she was no longer a child, and he waited for her decision.

'Your father — he will not approve,' she said at last hesitatingly.

He looked at her directly, his expression grave. 'I love you, Serana. He will accept you — for it is my wish.'

Her eyes filled with sudden tears, then she stooped and kissed his hands, 'I will gratefully accept your protection, Ischian — if you reject me now — I shall die.'

'I shall be proud to be your protector — yours and the child's.'

There was nothing more to be said and she smiled back at him. Together they returned to the camp-fire.

Once Serana had accepted the truth, she set herself to put thoughts of Egypt aside. She must now strive to become the wife that Ischian had longed for. He deserved her whole hearted loyalty and obedience, but try as she might she found it impossible to avoid her thoughts straying back to the country they had left. When they encountered a Midianite caravan on the tenth day of their journey, she learned that its destination was Thebes and she turned away into her tent, tears threatening to choke her, as memories of Raban rose up before her eyes.

How would he fare in slavery? Her tortured mind dwelt on the possibility of Pharaoh revenging himself for her escape on her helpless brother but she could not believe that he would really note her absence, or if he did, he would not care. There were so many other women in the harem.

Among the baggage was the bundle of clothes in which she had escaped. Vividly she recalled Nefren's room where she had changed from her shameless Egyptian attire. Gleaming dully in the light of the hanging lamp lay the gold and turquoise necklace. She touched its cold metal then snatched away her fingers as though it burned her. He had sent it to her, payment for the pleasure she had given him. Had he worn it? Her first sight of him had been dominated by the glitter of the gold and turquoise pectoral he had worn, his proud face above it frowning imperiously.

Suddenly she seized the necklace and clutched it to her throat. She knew what she had to do. The child she carried was his — belonged to him. She must go back. Ashtar had spoken of his longing for a child. Her child would prove to him that the gods had not deserted him. There would be others of course, later perhaps a royal prince borne of some foreign princess who would reign after him on the throne of The Two Lands — but hers might bring him hope again.

She would steal away from their own party. One of the drovers would help her. Already she had caught the boy's shy smile of admiration. He would take her to the oasis they had left two days ago, and there she would await the Egyptian caravan. The master would take her back into Egypt. The necklace would be her payment for his protection. She tried not to think of her betrayal of Ischian. He would understand — he must. She could bring him dishonour and the hostility of his household. Her child could never be accepted there.

Once in Thebes she would find out a way to stay alive until her child was born. Then she would seek out Ptah Hoten. The quiet gentle priest would know how to help and advise her. She could not approach the palace — an escaped slave. Even the thought turned her cold with fear. Whatever he did to her — he would not reject her child. Surely there would be a place for him in the royal household. There at least, he would be honoured for his descent from the divine blood of Ra — and perhaps, if he were pleased, he might let her rejoin her brother. Women did live with the slaves, she had seen them assisting their menfolk on the building site of the new city.

Many years later, Serana could smile when she recalled that it had never occurred to her once, to doubt that she would bear a son.

# PART II

PART II

# 11

Sen-u-ret threw two coins to an old beggar before she entered the pylon of the Temple.

'Come, Ranu,' she said, 'it is late and I wish to see my husband before the evening ceremonies.'

The old servant answered her in a grunt and she quickened her pace. By the sun's position in the sky, she knew she had lingered longer in the market than she intended and Ptah Hoten would be concerned. So intent was she, that she did not notice the huddled form by the pylon and when the woman spoke to her, she drew back startled.

'Please do not be afraid, lady. I mean you no harm. I am not a thief or a beggar. I just wish to ask if you live here in this temple.'

'Yes I do. What do you want? This temple is always open to those in need.'

'Does a priest named Ptah Hoten live here?'

Sen-u-ret expressed surprise. 'My husband is High Priest here in the Temple of Ptah. You know him?'

'I met him once. Would it be possible to speak with him?'

'Tonight?' Sen-u-ret frowned. 'It is getting late. He will soon be officiating in the evening ceremony.'

The girl drew nearer and Sen-u-ret noted her tired, drawn face. The priestess's trained eyes also took in her condition.

'You are in labour?'

'I think that . . . I am.' She bit back a small gasp of pain. Could I see the priest? It is urgent. I have spent many days looking for him.'

'Come inside with me. You need attention, that is clear. I am a priestess and can help. You are very near your time, if I am any judge. Foolish child, why did you not stay at home with your husband?'

'I have neither, lady, please, I do not beg — I can manage — I have work, in a vineyard near here, do not pity me. But I wish to see Ptah Hoten now, please it is important to me. It must be tonight.'

'Ranu, take the basket. I will help the girl inside. Lean on me. You need rest and help immediately.'

'No no, I can go back to the hut of my master. An old woman there has promised to help me. I wish to give you no trouble.'

'This is a temple of healing, dedicated to Ptah, the Giver of Life. Tending the sick is our work. Come with me. I would prefer for you to have our help rather than that of some ignorant woman.'

Serana was glad of her assistance. The pains

had come on her suddenly while she worked picking the grapes. At first, she had pressed on unthinking. It was too early for her child to be born. Many more days should pass before her full time was really close. If her calculations were correct she could not give birth yet. The old woman in the servant's hut had questioned her about dates and fixed the birth at least two moons ahead. When her work was over, she had once more made a round of the temples. She must find Ptah Hoten. It had not been easy. Most of the temple servants had been proud and aloof. No, they had no priest of Ptah. This ill-looking girl who was obviously some slave or beggar's brat was no concern of theirs.

Tonight she had tried this temple. As she approached, the pains returned. Her back ached and she felt sick and faint. The welcome shade of the pylon had seemed a refuge and now this young priestess could see her need, but she could not make her realise how important it was that she speak to the priest. She must know what he would advise, before the birth of the child.

Sen-u-ret led the girl into a small room in the healing quarter. 'Rest back on this couch. I will give you water. Try to relax. Do not tense your muscles. It will make the pains worse.'

'Please, lady, I beg of you, one word with Ptah Hoten.'

'Very well. Do not worry so. You are safe here. I will try to find him.'

Ptah Hoten was writing in his private apartment. He kept a careful account of all treatment, and wished to finish his notes before the evening service. He showed no annoyance however, when Sen-u-ret interrupted him.

'Can you come for a moment? I found a girl near the gate. She is in labour.'

'Summon a priestess to tend her. It is near the hour for Service.'

'I know but she seems very distressed. She asks for you by name and says she has been seeking you for some weeks. I think she may need special help. She looks very weak as though she has been straining and doing unaccustomed hard work.'

He sighed, 'And just before the birth. I will come.'

Serana gave a sigh of content at sight of him. This was the man whose serenity had once before impressed her in her need. He was the only person in this land she felt she could trust. She threw up a prayer of gratitude to her nameless god, that she had found him and by the signs, only just in time.

'You do not remember me, priest?'

He came closer, his healer's trained eyes noting her heavy breathing, tensed lips and swollen belly.

'On the barge. You treated the master builder, Rehoremheb. He had been mauled by a lion.'

He started and stared again at her drawn little face. There had been a girl, a Hebrew girl, he had thought, returning to the slave village in the Delta. So Rehoremheb was responsible. It seemed likely.

'I remember now. You assisted me. You were his mistress.'

'I was never his mistress, priest. He was kind to me, that was all. I must talk to you alone, please.'

'My child, this is not the time for talking. Let me examine you. You have nothing to fear. You may stay now with us until your child is born.'

'Please, I must talk to you.'

He turned. 'Sen-u-ret, wait till I call for you. The girl will not rest till I have heard what she has to say. Get servers and prepare for the birth. I'm afraid it will be a long and difficult labour, but we must be ready. It seems that I will not be able to officiate in this evening's ceremony. Will you arrange for a deputy.'

She inclined her head and hurried out. He bent over his patient. 'Speak, I will listen and examine you. Do not be afraid or embarrassed. I am a healer and accustomed to attending women.'

'When you saw me with Rehoremheb, I was escaping. I had run away from Pharaoh's harem.' He betrayed no surprise but continued with his examination. 'I had been captured in a raid. I was . . .' she struggled for words, 'desperately unhappy and some friends helped me to escape. I cannot name them, you understand?'

'Very well.' His voice was quiet, seemingly unconcerned.

'I was a virgin when I entered the palace, priest, I swear it. Only one man has touched me. My child is Pharaoh's.' He stopped his work now and gazed deep into her eyes.

'I am telling the truth. What am I to do? I dare not go to the palace. If you advise me to keep my secret, I will do so.'

'You wish to return to the harem? You find life unpleasant, now that you have your freedom?'

'No, no — oh God no — I wish to be free. I went to my lover, a brave and honourable man. He offered me marriage but I could not stay with him. I wanted someone who knows the Court to tell me, will he want his child, do you understand?'

'Yes, I think I do.'

'Do you believe me, priest?'

'Yes, I believe you.'

'Then tell me, will he want to know about the child?'

'Yes, I am quite sure he will want to know about the child.'

'Priest, I do not want riches for him. More than anything in all the world, I want to keep him, but he is not mine alone and they say he is concerned that he has no child.' She caught her breath and held back a cry of pain. 'I thought if he knew the gods had not deserted him, it would make him happier.'

'My dear, you must not concern yourself about anything more. I will deal with this matter.'

'Will they kill me?'

'You must not fear punishment. Lie quiet. You have a great deal of hard work to do, before this child is born. You must not worry about anything. Trust me and let us help you.'

'I can not be having my baby yet. It isn't time.'

He smiled wryly. 'It seems either that you have miscalculated, my child, or this child will be born early. Of this be sure, it will be in your arms very soon now.'

'What will you do?'

'Trust me. That is what you came to me for, is it not?'

'He would not have my baby killed?'

'Of that you need have no fears, I promise you.'

Ptah Hoten rose and calling a young priestess to care for Serana, drew his wife into his private room.

'How long is it since you visited the palace?'

'Some months.'

'Has there been talk of an escaped slave-girl. Think hard.'

She started. 'Yes, the last time I was there, Ramoses was in a right royal rage. It was the day after you returned with him from the Delta. He sent for me, you remember and gave me a present, that length of red silk. I have not yet worn it. It seems that he had taken a fancy to some new slave girl and given instructions that she was to be well cared for till his return. You know he never takes women with him on these expeditions. It seems that she had disappeared. He was furious. I was quite scared myself, I can tell you. He ordered the chief eunuch flogged, poor Bara, he sobbed at Pharaoh's feet and screamed he knew nothing of it. All the girls were questioned and some of them were whipped too. I felt very sorry for all of them. I've never known him to be so angry about a woman, not since Nefertari.'

Ptah Hoten was thoughtful. 'Did he mention anything particular about the girl?'

'No, I gathered from Nefren that she was a captured barbarian and that she had gold coloured hair and was unique among the women of the harem.' She gasped, 'You think that that girl . . .'

'She is a runaway slave. I met her on the barge of Rehoremheb. You will recall I told you I was called to treat him. The girl was hidden in his cabin. She tells me she fled to a lover who awaited her in the Delta village. She escaped out of Egypt with him.'

'She was pregnant then, that is why she escaped. Merciful Isis, what would have happened to her had Pharaoh discovered her condition . . .'

He shook his head. 'No, if Pharaoh took her she was a virgin. She would never have been offered to him, else, and in any case he would have known.'

'Then the child . . .'

'She says the child is Pharaoh's and I believe her.'

Sen-u-ret stared at him open mouthed, 'Then why did she leave the palace? He would have favoured her, given her anything.'

'It is possible that she did not then know about

120

the child and there was her lover. She preferred freedom obviously and took the risk of capture.'

'But, Ptah Hoten, why did she then return? What will Pharaoh say and do?' she shuddered as she spoke the last word.

'You know him better than I. What will he do? This girl trusts us and came to us for help. I cannot betray her to punishment or death. Will he forgive her and what about the child?'

'If he is sure, he will be in ecstasy. Oh I know him, Ptah Hoten. He longs for another child, he truly loves children. With them, he is himself. He will accept the child, if it is truly his and make a place for him in the palace, no fears about that.'

'And the mother?'

'I do not know. He will brook no disobedience and to prefer another man . . . I don't know.'

'She wants him to have the child so we have no choice. Sen-u-ret, will you go to the palace and tell him. He is fond of you and if you plead for her, I think he would be merciful.'

Sen-u-ret's sensitive face was clouded for a moment, then she swallowed, 'Like all of us, I am a little afraid of Pharaoh.'

'I know my wife.'

'I'll do it, though what I shall say, I do not know.'

'I trust you to do your best for that poor girl in there. If I am any judge, I'm going to have a hard fight to save her.'

# 12

Sen-u-ret threw back her hood as she entered Pharaoh's apartment and Nefren thought she looked agitated.

'Greetings, lady.'

'Is Pharaoh not in the palace?'

'Yes, lady. He is swimming in the pool.'

'Oh I see.' She moved over to an ivory chair and ran her hand over the inlaid design. 'He is not yet gone to the harem? Is he alone, I mean is he expecting . . .'

'He has not summoned a bedmate for the night, lady, not yet.'

'Yes,' she coloured slightly. Nefren stood silent, attentive, his arms folded.

'You wish to see him?'

'Yes I . . . Please, it is a private audience I want, otherwise I would have come to court to-morrow. It is rather urgent.'

He bowed and passed through the open front of the airy chamber into the garden. The ornamental pool glimmered in the light of torches. Pharaoh was alone swimming effortlessly, his royal robe discarded on the marble bench near the water's edge. He swam over and sat on the steps, as Nefren approached.

'The Lady Sen-u-ret requests a private audience, lord,' he said quietly.

'Now?' Ramoses reached for a linen towel and his slave expertly dried him.

'Shall I ask her to wait while I massage you, lord?'

'No, give me my robe. Tell her to come into the garden. It is pleasant here. Bring us some cakes and honey-wine. She likes the sweet stuff.'

Sen-u-ret prostrated herself at her cousin's feet and he gave a cool laugh, as he fastened the strap of his jewelled sandals.

'Rise, cousin. It is long since I had the pleasure of receiving you. Does Ptah Hoten keep you too busy at your humane duties?'

She coloured at his mocking tone and took a seat beside him as he indicated that she should with a wave of his hand. It had always pleased Ramoses to tease her. Even from childhood, they both knew her innate fear of him.

'You know well enough, lord, that our priestly duties at the Temple of Ptah are a source of joy to both of us.'

'True, did I suggest otherwise? Nevertheless I would like to see you grace my court occasionally. Marriage has diminished none of your beauty.'

She flushed again. 'You are gracious.'

He leaned back against the throne-like bench, his lips curving in a smile. Nefren crossed the garden and silently attentive, placed a tray, bearing wine, fruit, and cakes on a table by his side. Pharaoh did not speak, nodded his acknowledgement and sat on watching Sen-u-ret closely. She moved nervously and adjusted a fold of her robe.

'Well,' he said softly at last. 'What do you want?'

'My lord,' she protested.

'You would hardly come here at this hour of the evening and request a private audience, unless you wanted something very badly. What is it, mercy? Has Ptah Hoten robbed a tomb and been caught?'

'Don't be absurd.'

He threw back his head and laughed. 'That's better, a little less tongue-tied. I hardly thought so, but whatever is it? When Ptah Hoten wants temple funds he comes himself. Come, have some wine, it will loosen the tongue.' He sat up and poured the golden fluid into the lotus shaped goblet and she gulped a little, hastily.

'Do you remember my last visit?' she said at last.

'Yes, on my return from the Delta. You were at the feast of welcome.'

'Yes I was, but you sent for me earlier — gave me some red costly cloth, silk, I think you called it.'

'H'm, it came in the tribute.'

'You were angry.'

'I often am.'

'Please, I am serious. You had lost a slave, a

124

fair haired girl, do you remember?'

'Yes I do. My fools of officials had dared to let the girl escape. Her beauty was very rare. I had thought to take her with me on the Delta visit, and then changed my mind. I wished I had not, when I found she was missing.'

'You did not hear any more of her, she was not recaptured?'

A cruel expression deepened in his eyes. 'No. It would have given me pleasure to deal with both the girl and those who aided her.'

'Would you like her back?' she jerked out the question and knew she had, for once, his full attention.

'You know something of the affair?'

Sen-u-ret summoned all her courage. 'Would you punish her if she returned to the House of Women?'

'That question is superfluous. Of course.'

'How?'

He smiled. 'I would need to give some thought to the matter.'

She plunged on recklessly. 'You would have her executed? Please tell me.'

He stood up and taking the goblet from her, he placed one hand on her shoulder and with the other, tilted up her face to his own. She quivered under his hold and her lips trembled. She was mortally afraid of this man. He had never hurt her but she had seen him deal with others who had displeased him, and she had never once lost her dread in his presence.

'If you know where this girl is, or anything whatever about her, if you are concerned in this at all, you had better tell me about it, at once.' The last two words cut like a whip lash.

'I cannot.'

'Cannot? Do not trifle with me Sen-u-ret. I will not spare even you if you defy me. Where is she?'

'You are hurting me.' His fingers had dug into the flimsy material on her shoulder and she knew a bruise would form later.

'Do you wish me to hurt you further?'

'I will not tell you one word, until you answer my question. Will you have the girl executed?'

'I hardly think so. Slaves are valuable. I never destroy what is useful or saleable.'

'You promise?'

'What I have said, I have said.'

'A fair haired girl came to the temple this evening. She was ill. She asked for Ptah Hoten. She confessed to him that she had escaped from the palace some months ago. She is in labour at this moment. She says the child she carries is yours.'

He released her abruptly and stood quite still. She did not move, waiting for him to speak.

'Is it possible that she could bear you a child?'

'Yes.'

'She is desperately afraid for the child. You must understand, Ramoses. She did not return to Thebes because she wishes to become a pampered favourite, I'm sure of that.'

'I will come with you to the temple. Nefren,'

126

he called imperatively and the slave hurried out, noting the urgency of the summons. 'We go to the temple. You will accompany us. Bring me a cloak, a sober one. I have no wish to be recognised.'

Sen-u-ret saw that her husband was deeply concerned, when he came from Serana's chamber to greet them. He bowed low to Pharaoh and turned to her.

'You have explained?'

'She has indeed. I must see the girl.'

Ptah Hoten held up his hand. 'One moment, lord. I would advise you not to enter.'

An ugly scowl gathered on Pharaoh's brow. 'You refuse to allow me to see her?'

'My lord, you misheard me. Of course I can not refuse you permission to do anything. I merely said, as physician in this case, that for you to enter would be inadvisable.'

'But . . .'

'The girl is in a pitiable state. I am concerned at her condition. This will not be an easy birth. If there is any chance whatever, that this child is yours, we must put no difficulties in the way of its safe arrival. I trust you wish the child to live?'

'I would wish it to live, were it the child of any other.'

'Just so. I was assured that you would take this view. I propose to go in and give her a drink. She is in pain, I will offer her some wine compounded with a mild concoction of poppy. It can do no harm at this stage and will calm her a little. While she drinks it, I will command the young priestess on duty to hold the torch above her head. If you stand here near to this curtain, you should get a clear view of her features. For you to enter the room now will terrify her — she knows she stands in danger of dire punishment. Your presence will not help her.'

'I understand.'

'Now, I must make it plain that the girl may seem unfamiliar, childbirth often alters the features. She is terribly weak and half starved. She cannot seem like the girl who was brought scented and richly apparelled to your apartment.'

'It will not be so difficult. When I first saw the girl she was afraid then and her face was blotched and tear stained.'

Ptah Hoten threw him a questioning glance but made no answer. He signed to Sen-u-ret to hold up the dividing curtain and passed inside. When Ptah Hoten returned, Pharaoh's face was grave. He returned the priest's questioning look with a nod.

'Yes, I am sure.'

'It would be difficult under these conditions to be positive.'

'I am quite sure it is the girl.'

'Was she a virgin when she came to you?'

'Unquestionably.'

'Of that you are convinced?'

Pharaoh turned from him and moved to the other side of the room which was open to the courtyard beyond. 'Of that I have not the least shred of doubt.'

'The dates coincide?'

'Yes. On a rough reckoning I assume she spent some two months in my harem. She had disappeared on my return from the Delta. The last time I saw her was the night previous to my departure.'

'Ah, one thing only puzzles me. She continually states that the birth is too soon. It could be premature of course. The girl is ignorant of most matters of this nature, or so I assume. She could be wrong. She thinks this child was conceived on a night previous to your departure but that would make this birth almost two months premature.'

'It would and might still be correct, but,' Pharaoh spoke still with his back to them, 'there was an earlier occasion.'

'Then we can be almost certain that this child is yours.'

Pharaoh turned and Sen-u-ret had never seen such an expression on his face before. 'Ptah Hoten, brief as our acquaintance was, I know that girl. She was undeniably chaste when I acquired her, as you say completely ignorant and cold to the point of frigidity. I do not believe any man has touched her since. The child is mine. But how is she?'

'Her condition is poor. Labour will be protracted. You must be prepared to lose the mother and the child.'

'You can help?'

'Be assured I shall do all I can. She has made me swear I will do nothing to aid her that could possibly injure the child. She has overworked during the past months, driven herself almost beyond endurance. I think she is half starved. The chances are she is too weak to bear the child living. However, you must pray. The gods have not entirely deserted you, in spite of your denials of them. The girl has conceived. Take heart, what you have done, can be done again. If this child dies, you may yet give us an heir to The Two Lands.'

Pharaoh sank heavily into a curved chair. 'I will stay here.'

'You will not enter, you give your word.'

'Ptah Hoten, I am in your hands. I will do nothing to endanger the life of mother or child.'

'Let me show you another room away from the healing ward. There you can wait quietly with Nefren, perhaps even sleep. I will order refreshment for you both.'

At dawn Sen-u-ret brought refreshment.

'How is she?' Pharaoh's voice was made harsher by the depth of his anxiety.

'There is no news yet. These things take time. I warned you.'

'Is there anything I can do?'

'Nothing but wait and pray.'

'When my first child was born it seemed soon over. Nefertari screamed and screamed upon the birth chair. She cursed me and Egypt and all the Gods, but when it was over, she seemed as beautiful and strong as ever.'

'No two women are alike. Serana gasps with pain but she does not scream. It would be easier for her if she did.'

'Does she know I am here?'

'I do not think she knows anything very clearly. Part of the time she is delirious and talks of the raid when she was captured, then calls for her father and someone called Raban. She is afraid for him. Perhaps he was killed at the time.'

Pharaoh rose, 'No the brother is alive. Do you recall, Nefren, he attacked me and I had him flogged. I sent him to the mines or was it the quarries? Men-ophar would possibly know of his whereabouts. Find me a messenger, Sen-u-ret. This, at least, I can do for her. I will send for her brother and give him his freedom.'

'You must remember that we cannot promise . . .'

'I know that,' he gritted, through his teeth, 'but send me a messenger — fast.'

Through a bewildering half-world of pain and delirium, Serana floated sometimes unaware of her whereabouts, lost to sense and time. Abruptly she would come to herself to see Ptah Hoten bending solicitously above her and knew again the bouts of terrible pain which threatened to tear her body apart. She heard his quiet instructions and could only reiterate her plea.

'You will save my child. Do nothing to injure my baby. Please, he must live . . . he must . . .'

131

Over her closed eyelids he shook his head at the shocked face of Sen-u-ret. 'If this goes on, she will die. She is too weak to bring forth the child.'

'You could help.'

'It is always a risk. We could injure the child. I have sworn I will wait until the very last moment. We must pray. It is our only hope.'

For all their prayers, Serana's agony lasted through the following day and night and it was not until the early hours of that following day, when Ra had barely begun his journey across the sky, when the pain was almost beyond bearing, that Ptah Hoten spoke clearly through the mist of pain.

'It is time, my child, that we gave you some assistance.'

'No no,' she clutched at his arm, tearing the flesh with her nails. 'I will bear it. I must.'

'Trust me now,' he soothed and turned to his assistants who waited.

Through a crescendo of suffering Serana heard herself scream though she had fought them back until then. It seemed that an answering scream echoed her own. Voices rang out though she understood nothing. They were trying to tell her something but the mist was returning. She strove to push it back, so that she might plead again with the healer priest that he would do nothing to hurt her child, but the fog became thicker and drew her into itself.

Ramoses had left the temple and returned to

the palace during the day since matters concerning the state had claimed his attention. He had given strict instructions that he was to be informed at once of any change in Serana's condition, but since no messenger from the temple had arrived, he set out once more with Nefren in attendance to find out for himself. He was standing staring out into the temple courtyard when he heard the soft slap of the priest's sandals and turned an agonised face dreading the news he expected to hear.

'Rejoice, Royal Son of Ra, for the favour of the gods is with you. They have given you a living son.'

Behind Ptah Hoten, Sen-u-ret carried a tiny bundle wrapped in the linen cloth set aside for its purity in temple usage.

Joy fierce and jubilant flooded Pharaoh's soul but he feared to look.

'And the mother?'

Ptah Hoten shook his head, 'She has lost a great deal of blood and is very weak. I do not know. We must hope and pray. Isis surely will bless one who has suffered so much.'

'Don't you want to look at him?' Sen-u-ret prompted gently. She drew back a corner of the linen cloth and he peered down at the crumpled tiny face.

Ptah Hoten's half amused tones came to him as if from afar. 'If we had any previous doubts they are now dispersed. Those high cheek bones and slanted eyes are undoubtedly those of your son and no other's.'

He took the child from Sen-u-ret and held it possessively close. In sudden anger at being disturbed, its tiny face contorted with fury and it screamed defiance to the world.

'Give out your commands, little prince, heir to The Two Lands. We are your slaves and will obey. See, I hold you less tightly.'

'Heir?' Ptah Hoten's voice expressed concern. 'My lord, there will now probably be other sons . . .'

'Perhaps,' Ramoses smiled quietly, 'but this one shall follow me and wear the double crown; these hands hold the crook and flail of Egypt. Not in my reign will brother contend with brother for my favour, ambition seeping poison into the very air of the court. By sun-up Thebes shall know it has a royal heir and soon all Egypt. Nefren, summon a scribe and I will dictate, but first I would like to present him in the sanctuary of this temple.'

Ptah Hoten hesitated. 'Perhaps you would rather wait and ceremonially dedicate him in the Temple of Ammon.'

'When he was born in the House of Ptah? No, my friend, this child is under the divine protection of your god, and so I shall name him Mern-ptah, and in this name shall he rule all Egypt when I lie in Amentet.'

Quiet joy filled the heart of Ptah Hoten. It was known that Ammon was a fierce god and demanded blood sacrifices. It was meet that this child should belong to the gentle god of life, who seemed so miraculously to have preserved him during this bitter fight for existence.

'So it shall be written,' he said, 'by the will of Pharaoh so it shall be.'

# 13

Serana struggled vainly against the thick dark shadow which threatened to engulf her again. Vaguely, she could hear the sound of a fountain and soft, pleasant voices. If she could reach those sounds, she would be safe, but the great weariness of her body still insisted that she lie back and allow the dark cloud once more to draw her into itself. At first she was inclined to let it have its way and submit, but some pressing need forced wakefulness. She made a last pitiful effort and opened her eyes to find the gentle face of the priestess Sen-u-ret bending over her.

'Lie still, my dear, do not try to sit up. You are quite safe. You are in the Temple of Ptah, you remember? You came to us three days ago. We have been very concerned for you but the Gods be praised, you will be better now.'

Serana's returning consciousness struggled to recollect the burning question she had forced herself to wakefulness to ask. She gazed blankly round the room. She was lying in a small pleasant cubicle, one side of which was open to a shaded courtyard. It was from there that she could hear the tinkle of the fountain and further off, children's voices calling to each other in play. She turned anxious eyes on Sen-u-ret and forced herself upright.

'My baby . . . ?'

'The Gods have blessed you indeed, Serana. You have given Pharaoh a son, no you must not be afraid. He is very well — small but a strong and healthy boy. I will bring him to you in a few moments, but rest back, child, you are still very weak.'

The light was blotted out for a moment as Ptah Hoten entered from the shaded court. He crossed to the bed and took Serana's hands in his own.

'Now you must rest quietly. I command it.'

'It is true — my child lives?'

He smiled. 'Indeed he does and has let us all know of his presence. He has the strongest pair of lungs in the whole of The Two Lands. Sen-u-ret, I think we must let his mother see him, will you fetch him.'

He put a cool hand on her forehead, 'No fever,' he pronounced. 'Better — much better. Any pain?'

She shook her head, 'None but I can hardly move.'

'That is to be expected. You had a long and bitter labour but that is behind you now. You must rest and eat and grow strong.'

'Pharaoh does he know — about the baby?'

'He does.'

'Does he want to see him?'

'He has already seen him and is impatient to

take him to the palace nursery. Your son will be a mighty prince. Do not fear.'

Serana sank back. 'He believed that the child is his?'

Ptah Hoten chuckled. 'When you see him yourself you will know why.'

'They will take him from me.'

'No, no, why should anyone part a child and his mother. He is yours Serana, all yours. Ah, here is the royal prince.'

She looked wonderingly as Sen-u-ret placed the child beside her and moved the cloth to reveal his face.

'Is he not perfect? He is very good at the moment because he has just been fed. A young priestess will wet nurse him for you. She is perfectly healthy. She has a child of her own, but there is milk enough for two, for the present anyway.'

Serana smiled in spite of herself. 'He is very like his father,' she said touching his tiny fist hesitatingly. He immediately opened black eyes and stared at her defiantly. 'I thought that I would die. I wish in a way that I had,' but she went on wistfully, 'I wanted to see my child just once.'

Sen-u-ret looked horrified. 'You must not talk such nonsense. You have Mern-ptah to live for. Who will defend him and watch over him like his mother?'

'That is his name?'

Ptah Hoten nodded gravely. 'I am afraid in this matter you were not consulted. It was

Pharaoh's wish and he was presented in the temple, here.'

'I am content that he should be named for your God, Ptah Hoten.'

'It is well. Take the child, Sen-u-ret, and order some food for our patient. Pharaoh has sent over many delicacies and presents. When you are stronger, you shall see them.'

'No, no, I want nothing, nothing at all.'

'Child, you cannot refuse the gifts of Pharaoh.'

'I want nothing, only that he will care for the child, that is all.'

'Very well,' the priest straightened up. 'I will not plague you with them, however,' he paused smiling, 'there is just one outside that you may like.'

As she made to weakly protest, he held up his hand. 'Very well, but just one quick look at it, then you can decide if you wish to keep it or not.'

Serana sank back too exhausted to argue further. The priest crossed to the inner door. She could hear his voice but could not catch what he said, then weak as she was, she sat up arms outstretched with a choking cry of triumphant joy.

'Raban. Oh Raban, it cannot be.'

Her brother seized her in his strong arms as she sobbed against his chest.

'I thought perhaps after all, you might wish to keep this one,' Ptah Hoten said, as he quietly closed the door.

Later Raban went in search of Ptah Hoten, whom he found in the ward of the temple, attending a host of poor sick people who could not afford the services of one of the many physicians who had practices in the city. Giving orders to one of the younger priests, he rose and went with Raban into the courtyard.

'Will she recover, priest?' Raban's question was blunt.

The other shook his head gravely. 'I wish I knew.'

'But she is conscious now and knows us all. Is there still danger?'

'The greatest danger is that she does not wish to live herself. I think she had not considered what would happen to her after the birth of the child because she was convinced that she would die in the bearing of him. You can be our greatest ally in this matter. It is for you to make her want to live again.'

Raban turned away, 'She wishes to come with me back to the quarries to help with the other women. Do you think it possible?'

'Raban, Pharaoh has declared the child his Royal Heir. He wishes me to celebrate his official marriage to Serana as soon as she is well enough. She will be his consort, the most honoured woman in Egypt, mother of the Pharaoh to be.'

'Does she know?'

'Not yet. I feel now is not the time.'

Raban sighed heavily, 'Fear not, priest, I will be silent.'

For five days Serana lay in her small room attended by the priestesses ordered briskly about by Sen-u-ret. Ptah Hoten at last pronounced her out of danger, though he forbade her to rise from her bed. Childbirth had aged Serana. Her lovely bright hair had lost its sheen and hung lank on her pillows. Heavy violet shadows darkened her large eyes and her face seemed pinched and thin. It would be long before Raban looked again on the girl who had accompanied him to the wool sales.

The priest scrutinised her face carefully. 'You still look a little pale and wan, but a skilful use of cosmetics will repair some of the ravages. Sen-u-ret will know what to do. This afternoon you are to have a visitor.'

'Ashtar?' a smile sprang to Serana's lips. 'Sen-u-ret said she might come.'

'No, not Ashtar,' he said quietly.

He was alarmed at the sudden naked terror he saw in her eyes. 'Now my child, you must be sensible. Pharaoh comes to visit you formally to offer thanks for the gift of his son. He will make you presents of jewelry and offer his congratulations on your safe delivery. It is the custom. He has waited patiently until now.'

Her hand tightened suddenly on the coverlet. 'I am so afraid of him,' she said in a whisper.

'I know.'

'But how do you know?'

'I attended you in your delirium. You must be brave. This visit will be very brief and not for a moment will you be left alone with him.'

When Sen-u-ret came to her later, armed with an array of costly unguents and cosmetics, she found Serana, outwardly at any rate, calm. She chattered while she worked, arraying her in a clean robe of fine linen, combing out the lank tresses with a comb of fragrant sandal wood, a present from the Grand Vizier's wife, and finally spending what seemed hours on painting the thin, pale face to her satisfaction.

Ptah Hoten expressed himself pleased with his wife's work. He smiled encouragingly at Serana. 'You will not be afraid? He is here.'

'No.' Her fingers trembled slightly, but she forced herself to smile in answer.

'He will do all the talking, so do not be anxious.'

She could not bring herself for a moment, to meet his eyes. His voice was still harsh, but tempered with a note of anxiety, she had not known before.

'They tell me you are better, little mother of my son.' She looked up at him shyly, trying to hide her fear from those fierce eyes, the eyes which her own son bore.

'I thank you, lord. I am much recovered.'

'All Egypt shall offer thanks for your safe recovery. Nefren,' he called imperiously and she coloured as she met the kindly understanding gaze of the slave as he came forward to the bed and bowed deferentially. Pharaoh took from the box he carried a necklace of heavy gold, fashioned most intricately in a design of alternating bees, their wings outspread, and ears of corn, so delicately wrought that they seemed to have sprung from their stalks in the fields to join themselves with the bees to form the pattern.

'Accept this as a humble token of my gratitude, though neither words nor gifts can come close to what is in my heart.'

She steeled herself to the touch of his fingers as he placed the shining thing round her neck.

'You are not to concern yourself any more with the matter of your absence from my palace. It will never be mentioned again unless you so wish it, as for your brother, he may take his freedom, or if he wishes, I will find him a suitable position in my service.'

Happiness flooded Serana's cheeks with colour. 'You are good. My lord, if I might beg a favour . . .'

'My dear, you may have anything your heart desires when you are officially my consort.' He turned to the high priest. 'How soon will you perform the temple ceremony? I wish to be united with Serana in the sanctuary as soon as she is well enough. Our son's position will then be completely unassailable.'

Ptah Hoten was unwilling to meet Serana's eyes. He bowed. 'In two weeks, lord, we may fix a propitious time.'

'Good, see that the seers set a fortunate day and time. In the meantime, I will give orders that apartments shall be prepared for my bride.'

He took Serana's hand in his. 'You shall have complete privacy and we must find a trustworthy woman to act as royal nurse. If there is anything you want, you have only to name it. I have given orders that I am to be immediately informed. The next time I see you, you will be brought to me robed for your bridal. For some days I must journey to Memphis where matters of state claim my attention. Farewell, little one. Obey Ptah Hoten in all things. I leave your brother with you.' His lips brushed her fingers, then he was gone, followed by his attendants. She could hear his commanding voice instructing Ptah Hoten, until it faded in the distance.

She lay back and weakly gave way to tears. The cold feel of the precious metal round her throat appeared to be choking her. She attempted to remove the necklace but her fingers appeared incapable of unclasping it. Ptah Hoten found her crying quietly when he returned. He placed the sleeping Mern-ptah at his mother's side.

'You knew,' she whispered, 'all the time, you knew.'

He was silent and she stared accusingly up at him. 'Why did you not tell me? You let me think I should be free.'

For a few moments he remained silent then he said, 'Serana, why did you return?'

'I don't understand. You know why — the baby . . .'

'You *too* knew you could never be free. Do you really wish to be free of *him?*' He uncovered the child's face. 'You would leave him alone. Have you any conception of how he will need his mother in Pharaoh's palace; what jealousy, ambition, and cruelty, lie in wait for him; how many traps there are for the feet of the unwary? What will he do if Pharaoh dies? Have you thought of that? You have lived in the royal house, even for a short time. You know of the intrigue, hatred, fear that is breathed in the very air within its walls, and you would leave him to face it alone?'

She gathered the child to her breast, her tears falling on to his face. He made a protesting wail as his peace was disturbed, and she rocked him to sleep again in her arms.

'Hush, little son, I will never leave you.'

Ptah Hoten nodded content. 'When you made the decision to return, you sealed your fate. In your heart, you knew it. I do not think you can see it now, but *he* needs you too, and I believe that Egypt will come to bless you for other things besides the gift of an heir.'

# 14

Serana's heart thumped uncomfortably when Ptah Hoten came to her, after the women had ceremonially attired her for her wedding.

'How is it with you, little one?' he enquired gravely.

'I am afraid, Ptah Hoten, but I will carry it through, never fear.'

'Serana . . .' he paused and she looked at him anxiously, 'you understand you must spend the night with Pharaoh?'

She nodded, angry that betraying colour still flamed her face at the thought.

'You need not be afraid. He will be — considerate.'

She remembered little of the day's events. The temple was cool and shaded. Once out in the blazing heat, Pharaoh held her hand and the people surged forward to gaze on her. As one, they prostrated themselves and she was lifted into the carrying chair and carried by Nubian slaves through the streets of Thebes to the palace.

The great throne room was thronged with jewelled and painted officials. All eyes were focussed on the thin girl in her gilded sheath dress. She felt almost naked before their inquisitive, predatory gaze, as she walked to the throne-like chair standing slightly beneath that of Pharaoh's, which was hers for the evening as the feast was in her honour.

Her head ached and the room was stuffy. She was thankful for the attentions of the two Nubian slaves who constantly kept them cool by the motion of enormous feathered fans. Behind her sat the wives and relations of Pharaoh. She felt their envy as an actual physical force. She could almost hear their malicious tongues wagging.

She was thankful that she had been saved the necessity of entering into conversation with Pharaoh himself. Ceremony had prevented him giving her anything but an amused smile. Now all his attention was given to the court. She stole a shy glance at him. He seemed relaxed, almost gay, this evening as he leaned forward to speak to a Syrian dignitary. For once, the harsh scowl was absent from his features, the finely sculptured mouth alive with laughter. Nefren caught her glance and nodded, smiling. This was no ordeal to Pharaoh. He was a proud father, glorying in the admiration of his people. He clapped his hands at the skilled performances of jugglers and acrobats and instructed a slave to throw an array of coins to the almost naked dancing girls, whose long hair jerked rhythmically with the sinuous movement of their oiled bodies, as they threw themselves whole-heartedly into their performance, anxious to please their master on this great occasion. Nothing could anger him tonight, not even the fall of the tired, deformed clown who clumsily fell onto his divine feet. Any other day, this stupidity would have earned the slave a thrashing and the court held its breath as one man, while they waited to hear his fate. Serana could see the agony of fear in the man's protruding eyes, as he stammered his apologies in his harsh accented Egyptian. Pharaoh laughed lightly and waved him away.

'The floor is doubtless slippery with wine. Go away, fellow, and rest. You are tired.'

The man could hardly believe his good fortune. He stammered his thanks and bending, he touched Pharaoh's sandals with his forehead not once, but several times and thankfully withdrew.

The slaves plied her with rich food, fish from the Nile, fried in oil, roast goose, exotic fruits and sticky sweet honey cakes. She had no appetite, but ate a little at Ptah Hoten's gentle insistence.

The heat was making her headache worse and she swayed in her chair. Ptah Hoten drew Pharaoh's attention and he turned to her, solicitude for her well-being his first thought.

'My wife is weary. She is still weak from childbirth and must retire to her apartments.' He rose and offered his hand. The whole court bowed low as they withdrew and followed only by their personal attendants, moved along the corridors.

'I hope your apartments will please you. I have had my architects design a suite of rooms for you adjoining the royal nursery. There you can be private and secluded from the ceaseless chattering of the harem, which you know only too well.'

Guards bowed and stepped aside as the painted wooden doors at the end of the corridor were thrown open and he drew her within. The room was beautiful beyond her imagining. It was large and airy, the furniture finely made but tasteful. Soft curtains of transparent linen shaded her bed of sandalwood inlaid with ivory, its legs carved like the hoofs of antelopes. Along one wall, flowers and fruit rioted in a flood of bright colour and colonnades led out into the shaded garden beyond. Oil lamps lent their soft golden glow and with the brightness of the braziers near the bed gave the room a welcoming air. She caught her breath with the delight of it.

'It — it's quite beautiful, it is mine alone — really mine?'

'Yes, all yours. I must speak words tomorrow with your chosen slaves. I trust my steward has chosen wisely, however we must obtain a permanent nurse for the child. That must be our first consideration, but you like it? That is well.'

When Pharaoh at length withdrew with his attendants Sen-u-ret drew Serana to the bed. She took off the jewelled sandals and rubbed the wearied little feet. Serana was pleased to divest herself of the gilded ceremonial robe and jewelled head-dress. She took off the necklace, which had been his gift to her after the birth of their son. Attired in a gown of soft green linen, she rested back on the bed. A slave brought a cloth dipped in scented water and bathed her aching brows and she closed her eyes in bliss.

An hour later, Nefren tapped on the door and Sen-u-ret bade him enter. Serana sat up and looked at him enquiringly.

'My lady, Pharaoh hopes that you have rested well and requests your company in his apartments.'

'I will come.' She turned to Sen-u-ret, 'My son will be quite safe?'

'Sleeping soundly. All is well.'

Nefren said gently, 'I have a carrying chair, lady.'

'No no — I will walk,' she said hastily and he bowed again. Sen-u-ret slipped a light gauzy scarf round her shoulders and she preceded Nefren and two attendant slaves to Pharaoh's apartments.

He stood up courteously to greet her, as she entered, nodding to the attendants to withdraw. She tried not to look at the pillar where both she and Raban had received their punishments, or at the great bed ornamented with the jewelled disc of the Sun God Ra, surmounted by the outspread wings of Horus. He was still wearing his ceremonial robe, but had laid aside his heavy jewelry and crown.

'You are exhausted. Come rest.' He drew her towards a comfortable chair, then stopped abruptly and tilted her face up to his so that the light flickered on it and revealed her terrified eyes and tense lips. 'Please, my wife, do not tremble so. I swear by Ammon you have nothing to fear.'

She turned her face away. 'It is nothing, lord. I am tired after the feast.'

'You are afraid of me,' he repeated slowly and as she kept her face averted he said quietly, 'I tell you you have nothing to fear. Can we not at least be friends?'

She turned back to him quickly. 'Of course, you are very kind.'

'Then smile and relax. Do not start like a frightened gazelle, when I come near you.'

'I'm sorry, I . . .' she broke off, sudden tears springing to her eyes, 'I . . .'

'You have painful memories of this room. Shall I tear down the pillars and rebuild?'

She laughed suddenly. His explosion had broken down her wall of fear and he drew her possessively into his arms. 'That is better. But why do you laugh? Not that I would have you take it back, it was good to hear it.'

'The thought that you would spoil this lovely room, because I had been unhappy in it, seemed so absurd.'

'I would destroy the palace if I deemed it necessary.'

'You are serious?'

'Perfectly serious.'

'But that would be a dreadful waste of money and people in Thebes are so poor.'

His eyebrows shot up abruptly and she said

hastily, 'I have angered you.'

'By all the gods, no little one, but you say the strangest things. Am I to feed all the beggars in Thebes?'

'You are Pharaoh.'

He sat down and meditatively bit into a juicy fig from a dish near to his hand. 'Has it occurred to you that many of my people down there are irresponsible drunken rogues?'

She considered, 'No . . . but . . .'

'Most of the night they spend in taverns drinking barley beer and er . . . enjoying themselves,' he said with a twinkle as she coloured and lowered her eyes, 'tonight they will be in a drunken stupor at my expense — to honour you, my new wife. I owe them little more I think.'

'I am sorry, I have no right to judge. I do not understand.'

'You will learn. Our son must learn.' He rose suddenly, with one of those accustomed restless movements of his she came to know well. 'I will walk in the garden, perhaps swim, I often do in the cool of the evening.' He indicated the bed, 'Please sleep little one,' then turned as he reached the doorway, 'I shall not — disturb you.'

When she at last sank down on the bed, her emotions were confused. Relief mingled with a vague feeling of disappointment. She flushed hotly as she strove to define the sensation. Did she indeed desire Pharaoh's attentions? That was impossible. He meant what he said. Tonight at any rate, she had nothing to fear. He was concerned for her health, but honour determined that she should sleep within his apartments on their wedding night. The possibility was that he might never again honour her with such a summons. He had said he wished to be a friend. How could one be a friend to such a man? Ashtar could. She loved Pharaoh without passion. To do that, she, Serana, must forget Ischian. Could she do that? She told herself she must. The doors had closed on all happiness when she had left Ischian and could she altogether regret her decision when Raban walked free in the court? He at least was free to seek his own happiness.

When Ramoses returned to the room he paused in the doorway, then, as all was quiet, he moved to the bed and smiled down at the sleeping girl. He sighed and pursed his lips slightly at the evidence of tears on the pale cheeks, then ruefully grimaced as he threw himself into a chair by the bed hooking forward a footstool with one impatient foot. 'By the gods,' he thought, 'this is the strangest wedding night I have ever spent, and I have spent many.'

# 15

Serana found very soon that her position in the palace had indeed changed. When she entered the royal nursery, the slaves prostrated themselves to the floor. If she encountered a palace official in the garden, he bowed himself low. After the first timidity during the early days in the palace, she became accustomed to her new state.

Pharaoh himself made her slaves aware of it, on the first morning after her marriage. He swept in with Nefren after her women had bathed and attired her for the morning. As was usual each slave lay flat on the floor at his entrance and remained there. Serana rose and bowed as Ptah Hoten had instructed her. Now that she was a royal wife, a respectful salute was required of her not the abject obsequiousness demanded of subjects. She was a little embarrassed at the meeting. She had woken to find herself alone in the empty bedroom. She had been grateful for his forbearance but puzzled as to what her future position was to be in his household. He was soon to make it plain.

He walked slowly round the room, after first acknowledging her presence with a slight nod.

The slaves remained motionless.

'I have called to enquire of my wife if she is well served,' he said at last, coldly and clearly, 'if she has any complaints and to see for myself that the work is well done. If I am in the least dissatisfied with any one of you, that slave will be thoroughly flogged by my Nubians. I trust I am understood?' He swept into the nursery and she was surprised to hear his harsh voice soften as he lifted the child into his arms and moved into the sunlight whispering soft childish phrases to comfort the fractious prince whose slumber he had rudely disturbed.

She turned an anxious face on Nefren who shook his head.

'It was necessary, lady, believe me. Now they will treat you with respect and indeed it will ensure the safety of you both. That was essential. Come, Pharaoh waits.'

He turned at their entrance, making a charming domestic picture, the child in his arms. His pride was apparent. 'See how good his lungs are.'

'My lord,' the young priestess was deferential. 'Please give him back. You will squeeze the life from him.'

'Nonsense,' he held the squirming naked little body high above his head, 'he likes it, see he's stopped crying. Wait till you stand in my war chariot, little prince, then we shall know what stuff you are made of. Ah,' he turned, 'here is your uncle, let us hear what he makes of you.'

Raban hesitated in the entrance, 'Forgive me,

I thought my sister was alone.'

'Enter, I am glad you are here. I wanted to talk to you.' He handed the baby back to the priestess, smiled his satisfaction and indicated that they should leave the nursery. Serana was anxious. As Pharaoh threw himself into a chair, she and Raban remained standing and looked a little uncertainly at one another.

'What was it like at the quarry?' He shot the question abruptly at Raban.

Raban's answer was direct, 'The work goes well. I think they are making fair progress.'

'Man man, I didn't ask you that. I have progress reports frequently. I ask you as a former slave, not as an overseer.'

'I was not unhappy, lord. The food was adequate, the work hard but Tef-nut is a good overseer, not unfair. The slaves are content while conditions are good. Of course it is dangerous.'

'Dangerous?'

'Sometimes slaves are crushed by the weight of the stones or by carelessness injure themselves with the tools. Later, they become better skilled.' He gave a wry smile as he showed his maimed hand.

'It is what I thought. Conditions are not so good on all sites. Discontent could breed trouble.' He jerked up his head. 'Do you wish to return to your people or would you consent to stay near your sister? I could provide you with a position at court.'

'I would be delighted to stay in Egypt.'

'Good.' Pharaoh waved his hand. 'Sit down, my wife. You are still not recovered. It seems,' he gave his attention back to Raban, 'that you could serve me best on a commission to enquire into conditions of slavery at the mines and quarries. The copper mines in Sinai could first claim your attention.'

'The mines?'

'You would object?'

Raban hesitated. 'No, lord, I will go as soon as possible.'

'Good, that is settled.' Pharaoh rose satisfied that the matter was suitably concluded. 'I think your brother will be of great service. I must consult with Ptah Hoten as to the possibility of having a permanent healer on the sites. This would be an advantage, I feel.' He swept out to the low bows of the attendants.

After his departure, Serana sat down and looked questioningly at her brother. 'Raban, tell me truly, don't you wish to serve on this commission?'

'Indeed yes, it is an excellent idea. If I can help my former companions I will — that is if he really means to take notice of my suggestions.'

She wrinkled her brows slightly. 'I think he will do that. He surprises me so often. I thought human life was cheap to him. Now I am not so sure. He can be ruthless, but sometimes, unexpectedly merciful. You hesitated when he asked you to go. Did you tell him the truth about the quarry? Were you terribly unhappy there?'

'At the quarry life was bearable, but in the mines I would have gone mad had I stayed long.'

'And it is there he asked you to go first.'

'I shall manage to do the job. I,' he paused and gave a half self-conscious laugh, 'I hate to go underground. I suppose it is because all my life I have lived in the open. Even these buildings overpower me. When the master builder rescued me from that hell, it seemed as if my life began again.'

'So Rehoremheb kept his promise,' she looked away towards the garden. 'He helped me — well I must not speak of that.'

His questioning stare met with a shake of the head.

'Perhaps I can help those poor unfortunates who haven't sisters who please Pharaoh.'

'Oh, Raban, you talk as if . . .'

'Sister,' he interrupted quickly as he saw her troubled face, 'I am teasing you, but we must face facts. At the moment, he is prepared to grant you favours.'

She stood up, 'I suppose so, but I would not dare to ask for anything,' then she fell silent. 'You want something, Raban, tell me.'

'It is nothing.'

'Tell me.'

'At the quarry I met a girl. No . . .' He shook his head as her eyes lit up, 'it is not what you think, little sister. I met her only once and she is Egyptian. She has fallen on ill times and is so desperately unhappy that I wondered if perhaps, if you asked, he might let her serve you here.' He paused, 'It could be awkward though. Her father was executed for treason. He plotted against the life of Pharaoh. The girl was taken into slavery. It is the custom.'

Serana caught her breath, 'Poor child. I feel for her — to lose both father and freedom at the same moment as we both did.'

'Aye that is why I pitied her, though I imagine she was a spoiled little brat previous to her misfortune.'

Serana made up her mind, 'Do not fear, Raban. I will find the right moment to ask him — perhaps when he visits the child. We may have to wait. I will try. Her name?'

'Merya. She is a water carrier at the quarry. Her father was a captain in the army. Now I must go and you should rest. You look very tired still.' Serana gazed after him affectionately. She would miss him when he set out on his tour of duty.

One morning a few days later when Nefren called to inform her politely that Pharaoh was engaged in giving judgement and would be unable to make his daily visit to his son, she detained him.

'You mean he will try prisoners?'

'Yes but only cases where a sentence needs to be confirmed. Most minor cases are dealt with in the Nomes by the officials, but they cannot pass a death sentence for instance, that must be confirmed by Pharaoh.'

Her eyes widened in astonishment, 'Then he actually condemns all prisoners who are sentenced to death, in person? Nefren, can you tell me anything about one of the captains who was convicted of treason recently? He had a young daughter.'

'Senmut, yes I remember the affair. He was sent to the mines.'

'Are you sure he is not dead?'

'He was alive when he left the palace, of course.'

'The girl was sent to the stone quarry.'

'I believe so.'

'Nefren, I would like the girl in my service. Would Pharaoh agree, do you think?'

'You might ask. I should be careful. He is anxious about the child's safety and yours incidentally. He might not consent.'

'I would like to help. The girl would be happier here.'

'Possibly,' Nefren said cautiously. He rose and bowed himself out.

An opportunity arose to approach the matter of the slave girl when Nefren presented himself once more, later in the day. He bowed deferentially. 'Pharaoh requests that you dine with him, lady. It will be a small private party. The priest Ptah Hoten and the lady Sen-u-ret have been invited.'

Pharaoh was in a pleasant humour. Ptah Hoten noted with satisfaction that Serana was looking better. Her eyes were brighter, she was less tense and her hair shone under the light of the lamps. When she put on more flesh and her figure lost its angular lines, she would be a superbly beautiful woman. Her face had character and though she showed none of the passionate, slumberous fire of her dusky sisters in the House of Women, she was maturing. He realised that the girl had intelligence, hidden reserves of patience and wisdom, rare in a woman of her age and race.

When a young captain entered and whispered softly to Nefren, Pharaoh called him over. 'Come, what are you plotting? What secret matter must be kept from your royal master?'

'I simply wished to know about the slaves, lord.'

'Slaves, what is this, Nefren?'

'My lord, he means the slaves which were taken by the army. You were told this morning . . .'

'Ah yes, I remember, but I thought I had made it clear they were to go to the market for sale, don't bother me man. See it is done.'

The soldier saluted, his arm across his chest, and prepared to withdraw. Serana saw that Nefren was anxious to delay his departure. 'My lord,' he said quietly, 'if you will recall, you said you would consider the matter.'

'I have considered it. Send the lot to the market. We do not need them.'

To Serana's amazement, the slave persisted. 'There is a young chieftain in the company. He has been gravely wounded in the thigh and will be a cripple permanently.'

Pharaoh sat back, his brows meeting in amused bewilderment. 'Are you suggesting that I take a cripple into my service?'

'No one else will wish to do so, lord.'

'Nefren, you grow amusing, but I know you well enough to realise that there is reason behind this babbling. Be good enough to explain.'

Nefren hesitated and Ptah Hoten's slow beautiful voice encouraged him. 'Pharaoh has given you leave to speak. You wish to help this warrior?'

'I think he is a brave man who would work well in spite of his disability. He does not deserve to die.'

'I do not send him to his death.'

'If he goes to the market with the others, lord, he will be dead by morning.'

Pharaoh put down his goblet and sat up. 'I do not understand.'

'It is simple, lord, the slave dealers will not feed those they cannot sell. They kill off the sick, the maimed and the old, each evening after the daily sales.'

A spasm crossed the face of the priest and Nefren continued. 'He will not be bought as a house slave. He has no skills. He is useless at present in the mines, so he must die.'

'I think we had better see the young man. Bring him here, guard.'

The slave was a big man of about twenty years of age. As Nefren had said, he had been a fine warrior and leader of his people. This was apparent in the proud carriage of his head and dark intelligent eyes. His hooked aquiline nose betrayed his Bedouin inheritance, as did his olive skin. He had been bathed ready for the market and attired in a clean but brief loincloth. His hands were secured in front of him, but there had been no need to hobble his feet, for he walked badly and it was obvious that the thigh wound still gave him great pain. He obediently fell to the floor before Pharaoh as instructed, but the effort cost him further anguish and he caught back a gasp of pain. Pharaoh regarded him dispassionately.

'Do you speak our tongue?' he said at length.

'A little, I understand, lord, if you speak slowly.'

'How long since you were wounded?'

The man hesitated before replying. 'About a moon ago. It has healed but I limp, as you see.'

'You are a warrior?'

The dark eyes flashed. 'I was a tamer of horses, I fought when I was needed.'

'You are right, Nefren. He would be useless in the mines or the quarries in this condition.'

The slave lifted his face and looked fearlessly at Pharaoh. 'Will you offer me as a sacrifice to your god?'

Pharaoh's lips twitched. 'You would not be eligible since you are not whole. I do not offer my prisoners as sacrifices in the Temple of Ammon, though some of my predecessors have done so. However, you might be useful as a palace slave, possibly as an assistant to one of the gardeners.'

'I will try to please you. Lord, may I ask a question?'

Pharaoh frowned. It was not usual for people before him, slaves or otherwise, to speak unless directly addressed, but the man's attitude was not insolent and he nodded.

'What will happen to the others, lord?'

'They will go to the slave block. Some will be privately bought, others sent to the mines, brickyards, and the quarries. You have a companion?'

'My young brother was taken prisoner with me. He is scarcely more than a child. It was his first battle. I wondered what will become of him.'

'You are attached to him?'

The slave nodded. 'Since my father died, he has been more like a child than a brother.'

Pharaoh sighed and turned to Nefren. 'So be it. I imagine one more can make little difference. Could you train him as a personal attendant?'

Nefren smiled. 'Willingly, lord. I would be glad to.'

Pharaoh signalled to the guard. 'Take this man to the slave quarters. Free his hands. See that he is fed. Bring his young brother to my apartment in an hour. See that he is thoroughly cleansed.'

The wounded slave stooped and kissed the floor before Pharaoh's sandals. Serana was touched at this mark of gratitude. The man was no underling and it must have cost him a great deal to beg.

He rose and accompanied the guard from the room.

Serana felt a little uncomfortable when the guests withdrew and she was left alone with her husband, but he appeared not to notice and gave his attention to some dates and fine figs in a dish by his side. Having seen him in a mellow mood, Serana felt it a good time to petition him about the slave girl at the quarry.

'The Bedouin seemed very grateful, lord.'

'Let us hope he proves to be.' He looked up and smiled. 'Do not disturb yourself about the others. I will visit the market tomorrow with Nefren and question the dealers. I dislike waste of life or any other commodity.'

'Will the man be really useful, or is it merely kindness which made you keep him?'

'Buyers will not purchase maimed slaves, yet often an intelligent cripple can make a fine slave. In this case the temple healers may be able to tend the wound and cure him. It appears to have had rough surgery.'

'But you need not have kept the brother.'

He shrugged, 'It matters little to me and a great deal to them.'

She paused, twisting her hands nervously in her lap while he rose and drew together the beautiful dyed linen curtains across the window.

'Could I too ask a favour?' she said softly.

'Certainly, what is it?'

'It's about a slave. My brother Raban saw an Egyptian girl among the Hebrew women who tend the quarry workers.'

'Indeed?' He came back to her, his mobile lips parting in a broad smile.

'I'm sure it was not . . .' she broke off her cheeks flaming, 'like that.'

'No?'

'No. He felt sorry for her. He learned that her father had been guilty of treason. I . . .' she eyed him anxiously to see if anger had darkened the proud face. 'I wondered if I could have her as a personal slave.'

'You mean Merya, my captain Senmut's daughter. You may have her if it pleases you. It might be amusing for you to be waited on by a high-ranking Egyptian girl. I will send for her.'

'You are kind. Raban will be pleased.'

He tilted up her serious face. 'I am delighted to have pleased,' he hesitated deliberately, 'Raban.' As she flushed and lowered her lashes, he released her chin. 'And now I must send you back to your own apartments. I still have strict orders from Ptah Hoten not to overtax your strength, though,' he took both her hands in his own, 'I am anxiously waiting for you to return to health again. Good night, my wife. I will summon your attendants.'

# 16

Serana was surprised and a little doubtful when Nefren visited her three days later and requested that she sit in the hall of audience that morning to see Pharaoh dispense justice. He received her with a smile and the proceedings were a revelation to her, who had believed the man she had married to be a proud tyrant without sense of humour. Throughout two hours she listened to him deal cursorily with a landlord who had skilfully defrauded his tenant, wittily deal with a dispute between two priests from a Nome to the north, each accusing the other of hoodwinking worshippers by dubious prophecies, and dismiss a request for the death penalty against a young stone-cutter's assistant who had injured his sister's attacker. An elderly wealthy lecher well known to the court had seized the young girl and had her forcibly conveyed to his house. Her brother had broken in and rescued her, leaving the would-be ravisher half dead. Pharaoh lashed the old man with his tongue and ordered the immediate release of the girl and her brother, while levying a heavy fine on her attacker, which he ordered to be paid to the girl as compensation. The pair were too full of gratitude to express their feelings. Pharaoh turned and cast a mischievous eye in Serana's direction.

'The morning is sometimes tiring but never without interest. Many of these cases are dealt with by lesser officials but always I must listen to appeals.'

'Lord, it was quite fascinating. I understand penalties are seldom severe.'

His smile faded. 'Sometimes it is necessary to dole out severe punishment as a deterrent,' he said quietly, 'but fortunately this is rare.' He looked up as Captain Men-ophar entered, giving the royal salute.

'My lord, I can bring before you your new slave Ahmed, if you are ready to receive him.'

Pharaoh nodded. 'Certainly.' He gravely acknowledged the salute of Ptah Hoten who entered and stood quietly near a side pillar until summoned to speak.

At first glance the boy seemed unyielding, but there was dejection in the set of the drooping shoulders and Serana gave a little explanation of pity as she saw the lash marks on his back. He stumbled forward and fell before the throne.

Pharaoh regarded him fixedly, outwardly unsmiling. 'You are prepared to submit?' he said at last.

The boy nodded but did not speak.

'Answer me. I wish to hear it from your own lips.'

The boy's answer was low but audible, 'I will submit, lord.'

'Make obeisance before me.'

The boy hesitated. A defiant gleam sparked in his light eyes then he lowered his eyelids, stooped and kissed the ground at the feet of Pharaoh.

'So, you have begun to learn obedience. You will report to Nefren who will train you.' He turned to the priest. 'Perhaps, Ptah Hoten, you would send a young priest to attend this youthful sinner.'

The high priest stepped forward, his fine eyes for once snapping with anger though his words were cold but deferential.

'I will be pleased to tend the boy myself, lord, with your permission.' He stooped and lifted the fainting boy to his feet. Will Nefren or one of your attendants show me where I may treat him?'

Pharaoh signed to Nefren who led the way out of the hall. Ptah Hoten half led, half carried the slave in his wake. Pharaoh's expression was rueful. Serana had a shrewd suspicion that he lived in awe of the stern priest.

When Ptah Hoten paid his customary visit to Serana later that day, she questioned him anxiously about the young slave.

Ptah Hoten was grave but not concerned about his condition. 'He will soon recover. The lash wounds have been treated and he will be little the worse for the experience.'

'But he looked half dead.'

'He has been kept without water for almost two days.'

Serana's eyes showed her anger, 'But that was a terrible punishment and he is so young.'

Ptah Hoten shrugged expressively, 'I learned from Nefren that he has proved most disobedient. He must learn.'

'But in this way . . .'

'My dear, not only did he insult Pharaoh but also did considerable damage to his personal possessions and half wrecked his apartment. For this he received a severe beating and was deprived of water until he was prepared to behave. I cannot help thinking that considering the circumstances, he came off lightly. Nevertheless, I have treated him and he will soon be as boisterous as ever.'

Serana rose and crossed to a table where she kept the rolls of papyrus she was attempting to study. 'I do not understand Pharaoh,' she said, her voice perplexed, 'one moment I think him a wise and skilful judge and the next he reveals this cruel streak in his nature that I fear.'

'I am sorry for that.' They both turned at the dry comment, surprised to see that Pharaoh had soundlessly entered the apartment and was listening to their conversation, 'particularly as I have brought you a present. I apologise for entering unannounced, but I feared to waken the child. I know this is the time he sleeps.'

He did not wait to hear Serana's stammered explanation but threw open the door and gestured the guard outside to enter. He was accompanied by a slight girl of medium height, a little younger than Serana, dressed in the remains of a torn Egyptian tunic and a make-shift headcloth. Her eyes showed terror and she fell at the feet of Pharaoh, her head obsequiously lowered.

'This is Merya, the girl you requested. Stand up. Face the Lady Serana. Her appearance is pleasing to your eye?' He spoke about the girl as if she were not present. Serana nodded, taking in the girl's fearful expression.

'She has many skills. She will serve you well. Good, remove her. I will see that she is instructed in her duties.' He swept out, leaving Serana to sink down in a chair as usual feeling confused and disturbed. Ptah Hoten wisely passed no comment but quietly suggested that they resume their studies.

The slave girl Merya was delivered to Serana that evening by one of the harem eunuchs. She was dressed in a new coarse tunic, her hair freshly combed and round her dusky arm was the silver arm bracelet which proclaimed her a palace slave. She fell on her face before her mistress. Impulsively, Serana placed her arm round the girl's shoulders to draw her to her feet. She was alarmed at the girl's sudden sharp cry of pain.

'Child, what is it?' she said.

'It is nothing, lady, I have been whipped. I am sorry I cried out.'

Serana drew her to a stool and pushed her gently down. 'Whipped, why what have you done?'

'Nothing, lady, I am a new acquisition. It is always done.'

'What is always done? I don't understand.'

A wistful smile touched the girl's full lips. 'When a new slave is brought to the house, it is customary to have her whipped. It shows her what is to be expected if she attempts to escape or proves unsatisfactory. My father always did this and I often watched. Strange now, that I should be the one to feel the lash. I thought I should not be afraid, but I was.'

Serana did not know what to say. She would never learn to understand these people.

'I am sorry, now, that I asked for you. I meant you no harm, Merya. My brother Raban worked at the quarry. He thought you would be happier here with me.'

'You know Raban?' The girl's lips parted in sudden delight. 'Oh lady, how is he, well?'

'Yes, very well and he will be pleased to see you here. He is away on Pharaoh's business at present.'

'He remembered me.' The girl covered her face with her hands, a little sob of joy breaking from her enforced restraint. 'Lady, if you only knew. I was so desperate. It was not that the work was hard, though I was unused to it. The people were so hostile and the overseer's assistant cast eyes on me . . . He . . . he . . .' She broke down and seized Serana's hands in her own, 'I swear you will never regret asking for me. I will serve you till I drop with exhaustion.'

'I am sure you will, Merya,' Serana said warmly, 'I know I will be able to trust you. Now we must find you a sleeping mat and get you some food. Are your wounds dressed?'

The girl nodded, 'Yes, they tended me in the guard room. Do not fret, lady, it was not a severe beating, only,' her lip trembled, 'not pleasant . . . but I did not cry.'

'I hope you will have no further need to cry, Merya. Perhaps my brother Raban will find a way to let your father know you are here with me.'

The girl lifted her head, all colour draining from her cheeks. 'My father, lady, my father is dead . . . they . . .'

'No, Merya, your father is alive. He is a slave in the mines. His lot is hard, but he lives.'

'Lady, you do not torture me with hopes . . .'

'No, child, I have it on good authority. Your father lives and when I last heard, was tolerably well.'

The slave girl fell forward on to the floor, her shoulders heaving, the suddenness of her joy giving itself relief in a bout of weeping.

Serana placed a comforting hand on her shoulder and waited till it was over. She knew that the girl's loyalty was assured and in the fullness of time, she would be able to confide in her and find the companionship her lonely heart longed for.

# 17

Serana could not be more delighted with the attentions of her slave. The girl's gratitude was touching and their mutual interest in Raban drew them together more than might have been expected. Merya too was deeply afraid of Pharaoh and Serana knew that the girl understood her own unspoken fear. This desire to avoid angering him caused her to reveal to her maid the fact that his beautiful gift to her on the birth of her son had become accidentally damaged. The delicate clasp was found to be broken when she removed it from her jewel box one day. Guiltily she recalled that she had roughly struggled with it on the day he had presented it to her.

Merya examined it critically. 'Lady, there is no need to mention it, any skilled goldsmith can repair this in an hour or less. I will get permission from the mistress of the harem and take it to a worker in gold I know well. I can collect it later and it will be perfectly restored.'

'Oh, Merya, could you? I should be relieved. It is so lovely I fear he will notice it is missing if I fail to wear it.'

'Give me the box, lady, and I will go at once

unless you need me further this morning.'

Merya hurried through the corridors of the palace anxious to accomplish her errand and be back before her mistress needed her in the evening. She took a short cut through a passage which ran parallel to the private apartments of Pharaoh. While she knew well enough this was forbidden to female slaves from the harem she doubted if either Pharaoh or his personal attendants would be in the vicinity at that hour as it was the time of audience and he would be occupied in the throne-room. She was startled to hear in passing, a sudden cry, half angry, half afraid, then a sound of a crash. Someone would be punished for clumsiness, she thought ruefully. She halted when a gasping torrent of strange words met her ears, then a sudden panting breath, and most surprising of all, a low throaty growl, which could only have come from the throat of a fully grown lion. She turned back and peered curiously into Pharaoh's apartment.

Horrified at the sight which met her eyes, she raced in and fought with the terrified boy who was advancing on the growling lioness with a knife.

'No no, idiot, don't — give me that. What are you doing? Mu is perfectly tame.'

The boy turned green eyes on her. 'Tame, the beast is about to attack.'

Merya took the knife from his fingers and ran over to the lioness whose angry note had changed to a purr of pleasure at recognising a former ac-

175

quaintance. 'This is Mu. She is a pet of Pharaoh. See, she will let me caress her. You have nothing to fear. She has lived in the palace since she was a tiny cub and is quite harmless. She's just a great overgrown cat. She was captured as a cub. She has never been wild. If you are afraid I will take her away. The slaves will return her to the stables. She has quarters there.' She coaxed the lioness from the room and when she returned found the boy flushed and embarrassed.

'I thank you . . . you must think me a fool and a coward to boot,' he stammered awkwardly.

'Of course not. You were not to know. I have seen foreign dignitaries look askance at the beast, I assure you.' She followed his disturbed gaze to the small wooden table whose fall she had heard from the corridor. The boy picked up a small alabaster jar which had contained perfume. Its pungent fragrance filled the room.

'I knocked against the table in my fear,' he explained. 'I — I don't know how I shall dare to tell him.'

'He will be angry but he is just. Tell him yourself. He may have you whipped but that is soon over.'

He swung round, his eyes flashing fire, 'And pray how would you know that?'

'I would,' she said gently, 'believe me. I must go. I am on an errand for my mistress. I am Merya. If ever I can help . . .'

He smiled and coming over, took her hands

in his. 'Merya,' her name sounded odd in his accented tongue, 'you have helped me a great deal and I am grateful. Please . . .' He hesitated, and regarded her wistfully.

'Yes?' she prompted softly.

'Please, will you tell no one about . . .'

'No one, I promise.' Then she tore away her fingers and hurried away. Already she had delayed long enough.

She left the necklace with the goldsmith, who promised to give the work his immediate attention. As he assured her that it would be ready for collection in one hour, she decided to walk down to the river and enjoy the unaccustomed freedom from the confinements of the court. As she approached the quay, she saw a large vessel had recently been moored to the palace landing stage, a boat from the Delta, undoubtedly bringing some official from the new city. As usual it attracted the attention of a little knot of idlers; some fishermen repairing nets stopped to stare and a group of young apprentices, stone cutters by their appearance, chattered excitedly as they stood on tiptoe, striving to see the important travellers.

When she first heard her name called, she stood still, half inclined to run away. There were many people she had known from the old days she did not wish to encounter now, but to run was to attract attention to herself and that she did not wish to do. She closed her eyes and hoped the tactless one would retreat, but no, she was gently but inexorably turned.

'Little Merya, I thought I could not be mistaken.' She stared up at the impeccably dressed official. He was mistaken surely, she did not know him, but he had called her by her name. Puzzled, she looked up at his brown eyes then her lips parted wonderingly.

'It cannot be, no . . .'

'But it is — Raban! Little one you did not know me. I almost passed you. You look tidier than the last time we met.'

'Of course, my lady said you were engaged in work for Pharaoh.'

'I am indeed, I have just now returned from the building site where I have been attempting to draw up a report for him. I hope it will alleviate conditions. Let us find a tavern where we can talk.'

They spent a happy hour together. He was glad she was so happy and pleased that she would prove, as he had hoped, a loyal companion and attendant for his sister.

She questioned him eagerly about his work and he told her, with an odd reserve of mixed pride and shyness, of his endeavours to gain good conditions for the slaves. He had but now returned from the building site in the new city with reports for Pharaoh's attention. He was concerned for the safety of the old men and women whose task it was to grease the paths before the gigantic blocks of stone. Age and infirmity increased their danger as a sudden slip, or clumsiness in rising, often meant that they were crushed, as once the stones began their journey along the rollers, it was the custom of the overseers to allow them free passage and to refuse to halt them for any reason whatever. Certainly the fate of infirm and elderly slaves was not considered important enough to cause a delay in building progress. It occurred to Merya that she herself, only recently, had hardly considered the life of a slave of enough importance to warrant a change in any major plan.

She looked away from him, through the open doorway to the river. The sun was beginning to sink. She must return to the goldsmith's shop and collect the necklace. She parted with Raban with regret, instinct warning her that once more within the confines of the palace, her slave status would forbid free dealings with this man. He appeared not to notice her embarrassment and contentedly bade her goodbye, saying he hoped their paths would recross quickly.

The jeweller had completed his work well. She knew the man and had chosen him for his disinclination to gossip. He had been well paid and would remain quiet if he wished to do more work for her.

She had visited the shop many times before and turned quickly to her right where a small alley led away from the river and would form a short cut to the main avenue which led to the palace. Her thoughts were of Raban; pleasure at having seen him well and happy, and troubled that she was no longer free to consider any man.

She knew her way and did not even look very closely before her. Her direction was clear and this was a reputable neighbourhood, standing as it did, close to the palace, so she had no fear, as it was not yet dark and daydreaming, fell straight into the outstretched arms of the man who came out of the shadows and blocked her way. He placed one swift hand over her mouth lest she cry out and his other arm lifted her effortlessly in spite of her frantic struggles and drew her back into a small dark shop on the left of the street. She kicked and fought hard and he whispered urgently into her ear, 'Do not fear, lady. I mean you no harm.'

Once inside the darkened small room, he set her down and spoke again. 'I swear I will not hurt you. Promise you will not cry out and I will let you go.'

Merya was thoroughly frightened. She stared up into his face but could see little as the room was shaded, then she nodded violently and he released her arms and removed his hand from her mouth.

'Who are you? What do you want?' she said angrily, 'can you not see that I am a palace slave. You will get no money from me.'

The man's voice sounded odd, foreign. She could swear she had never heard it before in the palace.

'I saw you in a tavern by the river. You were with a man, well dressed, an Egyptian, one would have thought, but I could have sworn I recognised him as a former friend, named Raban.'

She started. 'You know Raban,' she said wonderingly.

'Then I was right, it was indeed Raban, in spite of his changed appearance. I could not be sure.'

She was cautious, 'His name is Raban, but I do not understand why did you not speak to him . . . If you are a friend.' Her eyes were getting accustomed now to the dim interior. She saw that he was dressed as a caravan merchant. He was bearded and his voice undoubtedly that of a desert dweller. She recalled now that Raban had spoken of his former life before his capture. He had been a Bedouin herdsman. She felt less afraid now as the stranger appeared to mean her no harm.

'I told you I was not sure that it was Raban,' he paused and seemed to be searching her face intently, then he said softly, 'he had a sister?'

'The Lady Serana.'

'Then you know of her.'

'I am her personal slave.'

He turned from her, and when he spoke his voice was husky with emotion.

'Tell me, is she well?'

'She has been gravely ill, but she is recovering. She has borne Pharaoh a son.' He appeared to evince no surprise then he asked,

'And is she happy?'

'Of course. Pharaoh has declared her his consort. She is the most highly honoured of the women in the royal house.'

'And you say she is content?'

'She *must* be content.'

He turned and came close to her, 'Lady, do you love your mistress?'

'I would give my life for her if need be,' Merya replied simply.

He took her hands gently in his own. 'Will you believe me if I tell you that I too love her with all of my heart?'

Terrified by the thickness of passion in his voice, she tried to draw away, but he held her fingers imprisoned.

'Sir, it is dangerous to talk so. She is the wife of Pharaoh.'

'I must see her.'

'That is impossible.'

'Please, I beg of you, I will take care. I would not harm one hair of her head by one careless word. It has taken me months to find her. You will take a message for me? I dared not speak to Raban in case I was mistaken and in any case, he was soon surrounded by Egyptian officials.'

She cut across his words, 'Who are you?'

'Tell your mistress the Sheik Ischian Ben Ismiel still loves her, waits for her, and must have words with her.'

Merya's dusky face paled. 'I tell you it is hopeless, she never leaves the palace unless she is heavily guarded. I am sorry for you, but you must go and never try to see her again. You will put her in deadly peril. Pharaoh would never forgive infidelity. I warn you, it would mean your death and hers and perhaps even my own, for complicity, if you were ever found together. Do you understand?'

'Yes,' he said gravely, 'I understand. Tell me, lady, have you ever been in love?'

Her fingers trembled slightly in his. 'I . . . I can not answer that, sir . . .'

'If you had, you would see my need and help me.'

'I will carry the message. I can offer you no hope, but I will try and bring you her answer. Tomorrow, I will find an excuse to leave the palace. If I am successful, I will come here two hours after noon. Await me here in the shop. I fear my message can only be "Goodbye", believe me.'

He stooped and kissed her finger tips. 'If she tells me with her own lips, that she is content, I will never try to see her again. I promise.'

Merya drew a deep sigh. She dreaded to even speak of this man to her mistress. The thought of Pharaoh's fury terrified her, but as she turned to go, the light from the opened door touched the face of the stranger. All sorrow seemed written on his grave features. It was painted round the eyes and etched in deep lines round the suffering mouth. Her heart was touched and she smiled fleetingly.

'I will tell her, never fear and I will come back with her answer whatever the difficulties,' then she was gone.

Ischian stared at the closed door. Some instinct

bade him call her back but his frustrated desires held him from the act. He dashed away sudden tears with his forearm and doggedly set himself to live through the torturing hours until the slave girl could return.

# 18

Pharaoh visited Serana that evening for the first time since his gift to her of Merya. Conscious that he had overheard her conversation with Ptah Hoten, she was afraid that she had aroused his anger, but he appeared undisturbed by the incident and seemed his usual courteous though arrogant self. Her embarrassed attempts to thank him for the slave were met with an amused acceptance. He enquired if she were satisfied with the girl and on discovering how pleased she was, professed himself content. He moved into the nursery and not for the first time, she found herself wondering what an enigma the man was.

All arrogance dropped, he lifted the child gently into his arms and sat with him peacefully content. The child had grown already used to his visits and no longer screamed in angry protest, but gazed unwinkingly into the black eyes above him. Serana knew that he would worship this father of his with blind devotion and her sad heart was gladdened at the sight.

When the priestess, who was still acting as royal nurse, once more took charge, he re-entered

Serana's apartment and seemed inclined to linger. Noticing the small harp on her table he enquired if Merya had displayed her skill.

'Yes, she sings and plays well, but she is attempting to teach me though I am a sorry pupil,' Serana confessed laughing.

'I see you have more talents than I supposed. I look forward to hearing you when you are more proficient.'

'My lord will have to wait a long time, I fear,' Serana returned quietly. 'I hear Raban has made you a report.'

'Long and detailed. He has given me a great deal of useful information. I can see he will soon be invaluable as an adviser in this capacity. He has visited you?'

'Briefly after he left you. He has promised to come again tomorrow.'

'I hope he duly noticed the slave girl he took such a fancy to. By the way, where is the dusky beauty, this evening?'

'Oh, I sent Merya into the city on an errand,' Serana hoped he would not notice her flushed guilty countenance, 'she will report to me soon, I am sure.'

'Do not allow her too much freedom. She was a spoilt child. I know Merya. Like my lion cub Ahmed, she will need schooling.'

'I understood it had already been done,' Serana's voice expressed her disapproval.

His raised eyebrow showed that her distaste had been noted. 'Simply a precaution,' he said

186

mildly, though a gleam she knew well appeared in his eye.

'And the boy, Ahmed, how is he taking his schooling?' she heard herself foolishly plunge on, though she could have bitten her tongue with vexation at once more mentioning the bone of contention between them.

'He is learning and I assure you, he took no great harm from the lesson and nor do I see, did Merya,' he smiled as the slave girl slipped in through the door. Merya stood stock still for a moment, then recollecting herself, came forward and threw herself at his feet.

'Rise, child,' he said quietly, 'I trust you performed your errand satisfactorily.'

Serana looked quickly at the girl who rose and stood, head bowed, at his command.

'I sent her to the jeweller's,' she said hurriedly.

'Something you wish to buy? I will see to it that it is sent to you at once.'

'No, no, just a slight repair.'

'I see,' he rose satisfied. 'Well, I will return to my apartment and see if Ahmed has managed to break any more of my possessions. I had ordered some new perfume and meant it as a gift for you, but the clumsy child knocked it from the table. However, he had the grace to confess, so I contented myself with sending him to bed without food.'

Merya started and looked at him intently. 'You wish to say something?'

'No, lord,' she said, flushing darkly.

'You knew about this? Come speak.'

'Ahmed was startled by Mu, lord. It was a pure accident.'

'Ah, I begin to see daylight. If he were not prepared my lioness would indeed cause a momentary shock.' He rose, 'I will leave you to discuss your women's secrets alone.'

After his departure, Merya drew a quick gasp of relief and gave into Serana's hands the necklace. 'It's perfectly restored, lady. Here is the rest of the money you gave me.'

Serana waved it impatiently away, 'Keep it, child.'

'Lady, are we quite alone?'

Serana looked at her sharply. 'Yes, I think so. Close the doors into the nursery and come close. What is it, Merya?'

Merya examined the room swiftly. On satisfying herself that they could not be overheard, she sat down at her mistress's feet. 'Sometimes I think that man has supernatural power. How else could he know I have a secret to impart to you,' she grumbled softly.

'Secret, but the necklace . . .'

'Lady, I do not mean the necklace. I bear a message to you from the Sheik Ischian Ben Ismiel.'

Serana suppressed a startled cry. Merya looked up into her terrified face and quietly related her story. Serana paced the floor, while her maid silently watched from her crouching position near her chair.

'The fool. He will place himself in danger. I have nothing to say to him. I cannot see him.'

'Lady, I believe he loves you well.'

Serana stood still and gazed down into the slave's dark eyes. 'Too well,' she said brokenly, 'I should not have dealt him such a blow.'

'You love him?' Merya's words were whispered but Serana caught them.

'No — of course not — I . . . I . . . don't know . . . I can't . . .'

'You must send a message. I have promised to visit him tomorrow.'

'Child, it is dangerous.'

'Lady, I think it would be more dangerous to leave him without word. He is desperate.'

Serana nodded and bit her lip, one hand clenching anxiously the carved wooden arm of the chair. 'Tell him I wish him well, but he must leave Egypt and seek a wife among his own people. There is nothing else I can say.'

'He asks if you are content.'

Serana lowered her eyes. 'Tell him I am — content.'

Merya's own eyes were troubled as she watched her mistress's back, then she rose and picked up the necklace, 'Do not despair, lady, I will see him.'

Serana placed her hands on the girl's shoulders. 'You will take care?'

'Surely, lady, do not fear. I have learned discretion in a hard school.'

Merya found Ischian in a state of restless despair. She had been delayed somewhat by an unexpected visit of Pharaoh to Serana's apartment. It was decided that she should go into the city, this time to buy some perfumed oil required for the bath, but as she was about to make arrangements to leave the women's quarters, Pharaoh arrived and etiquette demanded that no one should leave.

Serana was herself a little doubtful about the reason for his appearance, but he seemed in a good humour. As usual he made first for his son's nursery, then seated himself comfortably in a chair in her own apartment.

'Now that you are recovering, I am thinking of making a Nile journey down river to Memphis. There are several matters which need my attention and I wondered if you might — accompany me this time. The child is thriving and can be safely left now, I think. You have seen little of the country and travelling on the royal barge is perfectly comfortable even luxurious. Would you find such a journey tiring? The weather will soon be pleasantly cooler. Shall I consult Ptah Hoten as to the advisability of you taking the trip?'

The prospect of freedom from the overpowering restraint of the harem, filled Serana with delight. Her eyes brightened and she spoke impulsively. 'I would like it exceedingly, if you are sure I will be no trouble.'

'No, indeed, it will give the people an opportunity to see you, but I do not think you will find the ceremony too exhausting.' He dismissed the matter as settled and stayed to talk for a while.

For this reason it was about an hour later than she had promised, that Merya knocked softly on the door of the shop in the street of the gold-smiths. Ischian drew her inside, his eyes tortured with doubts.

'It is late. I was beginning to think you would not keep your word.'

Hurriedly Merya explained the reason. At the mention of Pharaoh the anguish deepened in his dark eyes.

'She will see me?'

'Sir, it is impossible. She says that she wishes you well and thanks you for past kindness, but that you must return now to your own people and forget her.'

'I cannot,' he turned on his heel and the words were forced out in a harsh cry. 'I will not go till I see her. I shall know if she is content and not lying. If I am sure, I will do what she wishes and never try to see her again. Tell me — do no men ever enter the women's quarters?'

'Only the priests who are healers, Pharaoh himself and his guards and officials.'

'Is the harem guarded?'

'Most strictly — inside by eunuchs and female slaves, outside by a contingent of the royal house-hold guards.'

Ischian's lip twisted wryly. 'I could hardly pass as any of those — no other men enter, you are sure, what about tradesmen or confectioners, craftsmen?'

191

'Very rarely. Most of the women buy their trinkets here in the city or are given them as presents. All the household servants and suppliers are known well by the eunuchs. Occasionally we get a pedlar selling silks or perfumes,' she paused and he watched her anxiously till she resumed, 'it would be a terrible risk. I could not guarantee that you could see her alone.'

'Tell me.'

'We are short of supplies of perfumed oils and unguents. This is the excuse I have used to leave the palace. I will show you what to buy and recommend you. They might let you in to show your wares to the women but . . .'

'But . . . ?'

'I warn you, if you are discovered it would mean your death and a terrible one. Swear to me, that if caught, you will never allow the name of Serana to cross your lips.'

'Do you believe that I would?'

She shook her head impatiently, 'It is not so simple as you believe. They would torture you.'

'I know it.'

'Then come. I will show you some shops where you can purchase a supply of the oils and perfumes. Have you money? They will be costly and you may have to bribe the eunuchs to allow you to enter. The women's quarters are on the left of the palace. Explain to the guards at the main gate. If they allow you to proceed further, they will tell you where to go. Come tomorrow, two hours after noon. Do not delay too long if that is not possible. Today Pharaoh told my lady he purposed to visit Memphis and take her with him. I will try to arrange it that at that time tomorrow, you are alone together in her apartments.'

Thebes was crowded as usual as she led him swiftly towards the shopping quarter and pointed out various booths where he might buy the sweet-smelling commodities so beloved of Pharaoh's bevy of women, sweet-scented oil, unguents, eye paints, malachite and all the paraphernalia of the lengthy toilet.

'I must go and buy what I need in this shop. Wait for me, then enter yourself and purchase what you need. Choose the best, the palace demands it, and insist on expensive containers. These fripperies the women love.'

She touched his hand fleetingly, 'You will not need to change your appearance. None know you in the palace save the lady Serana, and merchants such as you often come from the caravan routes. Your god go with you.'

He stooped and taking her wrist, he kissed it gently. She stared up at him, surprised by the gesture and he withdrew a little embarrassed. Indeed, he could not have told why he had touched her thus. As she entered the shop, he withdrew into the shade offered by a tamarisk. He must not approach this girl again, for her own safety. If his motives were distrusted by the palace officials, she must not appear to be involved.

The shopkeeper produced a small jar of Serana's favourite bath oil, but expressed regret that he had little in stock.

'Indeed, lady,' he said deferentially bowing to Merya whose arm bracelet proclaimed her a palace slave, 'I would have sent my regular supply to the palace, but I am waiting for a large order to arrive. The caravan from Midian is late. I fear a sandstorm in the desert may have caused delay or even death to my usual suppliers. However, I have this, unless you would wish to try another.'

'No, this should do well, until your suppliers arrive.' Merya paid for the oil and withdrew. There was no sign of the young sheik, so she concluded he deemed it best to keep clear of her in the future. She was a little thoughtful. If supplies were short, Ischian would have to search several shops before obtaining what he required. She trusted he would take the necessary steps and find his own source of supply and she turned towards the palace. She was deep in thought when she was hailed and turned to find the young slave, Ahmed, hurrying to catch her up.

'You walk like a young warrior,' he said panting. 'I called you when you went into the shop. I don't think you heard me.'

'I am sorry. I was hurrying back to the palace. It will soon be time for my mistress to dress for the evening. She will need this.'

'I will walk with you.' He fell into step beside her, his light eyes eagerly noting the colour and confusion of the street. 'I was allowed my freedom for the first time but I must be back soon. I too must assist Nefren to robe Pharaoh. There is a banquet tonight.'

'I hear you were not too heavily punished yesterday.'

He smiled. 'I was not punished at all. Someone told Pharaoh of the lioness. He was amused but he sent a slave with some food for me.'

'So someone proved useful.'

'You promised you would say nothing — however I was grateful for your advice. It was not so difficult to confess as I had thought.' He hesitated, 'Are you ill-used or is your mistress kind to you?'

Merya smiled. 'Very kind. I love her very much, but I am Pharaoh's property, as you are and I know well what it is to feel the force of his anger. He had me whipped on arrival.'

He looked up at once. 'I can see now why you understood. He is a strange man. I hate and fear him yet . . .' he broke off and shrugged, 'do you know he arranged for my brother to be treated by the temple healers? He had been wounded and it had festered. Now he has no pain and hardly limps at all. Why should Pharaoh do that for a slave?'

'Why not? A slave is useful. Yes, he is a good master, but take my further advice and anger him no more. His fury is a terrible thing. I have seen it. I know.'

The boy's eyes narrowed as he watched her intently, then she laughed merrily and hurried from him to the women's quarters.

# 19

Ischian found it extremely difficult to buy the expensive commodities he required. He followed Merya's advice and insisted on the finest that could be obtained, but due to shortage of supplies, he was forced in the end, to seek a caravan lately arrived in Thebes and from the merchants, he equipped himself with pots and jars beautiful and costly enough to please the most pampered and spoilt darling of the harem.

He spent a sleepless night during which doubts assailed his mind as to the advisability of continuing with the plan. In the morning however, the sun's rays brightened the sky and seemed to put his fears into perspective. He lived in a fever of restlessness until Ra climbed to his full height and he knew that it was noon. He prepared to set out for the palace. It was full early but even so he could contain himself no longer and he could perhaps obtain some idea of the guards at the gate by observing them from a distance.

It was, after all, a simple matter to gain admittance. The two young men on duty quipped him about his beard and outlandish appearance, but on learning his business, good humouredly gave directions to the House of Women and sent him on his way. The harem eunuchs were not so trusting however. The flabby huge Negro questioned him carefully and consulted with the harsh-faced mistress of the harem, before grudgingly allowing him inside. He showed his wares but not until he offered them gold did cupidity gleam in their eyes and they finally allowed him access to the large airy hall where Pharaoh's lesser concubines and slaves spent their hours gossiping and amusing themselves.

They launched themselves upon him, chattering and screaming like some of the strange raucous and gaudy birds he had seen on sale in the city. Masking his confusion, he bowed his head to the boxes he carried and prepared to display his wares.

If he had been concerned about his lack of bargaining power, he need not have worried. The women noticed nothing odd in his behaviour. They pressed him, with little cries and claps, to show what he carried, then argued and fought over the exquisite little containers, as though they had never seen such wares before.

When the chattering and screaming abruptly stopped, he looked up to find the harem mistress, standing, head lowered, by the side of a tall man who had entered unannounced. The women at once prostrated themselves and he knew he was in the presence of Pharaoh. He was unable to look full at the man he had wondered about for so long, forced as he was to keep his head respectfully lowered. He was not surprised at the ringing tones of the gold-like one's voice.

'I see I need not enquire into your state of well-being. You all seem in excellent health.'

Under his lashes, Ischian saw the women sit up and like children anxious to please, each girl in her own way, arranged herself to best advantage to please her master.

'So this merchant brings you new toys. The voice was half amused but indulgent.'

The harem mistress Fer-nut felt called upon to explain.

'We have not received our customary supplies of perfumes, lord. I thought it would please the ladies to see this merchant's goods.'

'By all means. I will pay for what they require. See to it.' He gave a swift glance round the room, turned to depart, then with a lightning move the women knew well, he turned abruptly to Ischian. 'Visit my apartment later. I will send a guard. I too would buy from you if your goods please me.' He stooped and lifted a small alabaster jar from a table then turned and left the room.

Ischian was content to allow the women freedom to examine his wares while he strove to order his thoughts. How could he be sure of being allowed to visit the royal wife? Merya had explained that Serana had private apartments of her own. He knew that Ashton too, enjoyed this privilege, but so far, no mention had been made of these ladies of exalted rank.

Pharaoh was amused as he strolled back to his

own apartments. The trifling amount the perfumes would cost him would be easily offset by the peace that would prevail for a while in the women's quarters. He paused for a moment before entering his own apartment, to breathe in the scented air from the garden. The cool season now had begun and it was much pleasanter to walk abroad in the city. The Nile was rising and river traffic once more was able to proceed up and down stream as business demanded. He was quite looking forward to the proposed trip to Memphis.

Nefren and Ahmed were busy inside. He could hear Ahmed's accents clearly. The boy was fond of Nefren and chattered unceasingly, boasting boyishly about his former position in his homeland and of his many exploits.

'She is pretty, the slave girl Merya. I imagine many men admire her.'

Nefren's voice was faintly amused. 'The Lady Merya is not for you, you young dog. She is still very young.'

The boy's laughter was genuine. 'No, Nefren, you wrong me. I like her, that is all. I can talk to her and she understands. I saw her in the city yesterday, I wondered if she had gone to meet a friend.' He dropped his voice to a conspiratorial whisper, 'I saw her with a tall Bedouin, they seemed very intent on their conversation and at the end, he kissed her, rather strangely I thought. Anyway, she took care not to mention him when I caught her up and I thought it best not to question her about him. I saw him near the women's quarters just now. Perhaps he wants another glimpse of his sweetheart.'

Pharaoh did not catch Nefren's answer. A perplexed frown crossed his brow; Merya and a desert dweller, the man he had seen even now selling his wares! It did not make sense. That man would never have attracted the mischievous and flighty Merya he remembered, young officers and noblemen yes, but he could not see Merya engaging in an illicit love affair with a grave solemn man such as the stranger appeared to be. She had been in the city. He recalled now that she had seemed ill at ease, when she found him present with her mistress, on her return. Serana had been very quick to give an explanation. Had the look he had discerned on the girl's face been that of guilt?

He moved abruptly inside and caught Ahmed by the wrist. 'You say you saw the slave Merya in conversation with the merchant who is selling perfumes in the harem?'

The boy was taken by surprise and flushed hotly. He was alarmed at the possibility that he had caused trouble for his friend by his aimless gossip. 'No, lord, I was perhaps mistaken,' he stammered, 'I was not close.'

Pharaoh's tones were silky, 'Come now, Ahmed, I should not like you to lie to me — you saw them together, yesterday. Where?'

'She came from a shop. It sold perfume and myrrh and spices, I think.'

'And they kissed?'

'Oh no, they did not embrace. He kissed her wrists, very gently, as if he were thanking her for something.'

Pharaoh released the boy and his ugly scowl changed to a smile, though Nefren noticed it did not reach the eyes, which glittered in a way which alarmed him. 'You may go. I shall not need you again for some time.' He moved to a table and his fingers beat a swift tattoo on its surface. 'Ask Captain Men-ophar to bring the merchant here to my apartment. I think it is time we took a closer look at him. I think our Merya is up to something and I would like to know what it is.'

Ischian had the grim foreboding things were going very wrong when he lifted his head from his deep obeisance in Pharaoh's presence and encountered the glitter in those dark, unfathomable eyes. For a few moments they regarded one another steadily. This then, was the man who had possessed Serana's body and was the father of her child. Ischian noted the strange, unusual beauty of the dominating face, the wide noble brow, the scornful, perfectly chiselled lips. Only fear could prevent a woman from worshipping this man. Power was latent in every inch of his being. Ischian had never been afraid before in his life, but he felt panic welling up within him from the innermost part of his being and strove to keep his lips from trembling.

'And where do you come from, merchant?'

Serana had told him little of this man. Even this strange harsh voice she would never be able

201

to forget, Ischian thought, while he strove to collect his thoughts, to weigh carefully his answers. He bowed.

'I come from a caravan from Midian, lord. Hearing that there was a shortage of oils and perfumes in the palace, I thought I might make a small profit in their sales here. The guards obligingly admitted me, on hearing my business. I trust they were not at fault.'

'No,' the dark eyes continued to watch him carefully and Pharaoh leaned back in his carved chair, outwardly relaxed, though Ischian had the strange feeling that he was very much on the alert, 'no, that was quite permissible, provided your intentions were honest, of course.'

Ischian could find no answer to this and inclined his head deferentially.

'From whom did you hear of the shortage?'

Ischian gazed back at him blankly, 'It was being discussed in the city, lord. I thought it common knowledge.'

'Possibly from a slave girl, Merya?'

'I do not recall the name.'

'Strange,' the dark eyes mocked him, 'you do not usually enquire the name of a girl with whom you spend hours in conversation and kiss at parting?'

Ischian tried to think quickly. Had the girl betrayed them? He could not think this likely. 'Your informant must be mistaken, lord.'

Pharaoh said nothing. He unscrewed the stopper from the alabaster jar he had taken with him from the women's quarters and sniffed it carefully, then held it out to him.

'Your finest wares?'

'Of excellent quality, lord, I assure you.'

His interrogator leaned forward suddenly towards him, smiling blandly. 'You have been cheated, merchant. This is of poor quality, suitable for a minor official's wife or even a noblewoman who was not discerning in her taste, but to offer to Pharaoh or the women of this court, never. Where did you obtain such inferior wares, or was your intention merely to cheat?'

Ischian took the proffered jar. He knew nothing of such matters. The caravan master had charged him highly and assured him of the quality of the merchandise. He hesitated but was interrupted by a voice which cut like a whip.

'You have an interest in some woman of my household.'

'No, my lord.'

'A desert dweller, like yourself. It should not be difficult to find the answer to this question.'

'I swear you wrong me . . .'

'Captain Men-ophar, ask the Lady Serana to visit me now, in my apartments. See that Merya accompanies her.' As if he had no further interest in the merchant, Pharaoh waved him away and gave his attention to some rolls of papyrus on a table by his side.

Serana was puzzled by Captain Men-ophar's request. He found her nursing her little son. At his grave expression, she handed him to his nurse and calling Merya to follow, accompanied him as bidden. She was totally unprepared for what she saw. Afraid of her mistress's disapproval, Merya had thought it best not to tell her of the plan. Serana swept into the room to stare into the anguished gaze of Ischian Ben Ismiel. Unable to prevent herself, she cried out his name and moved towards him. The ominous silence told her of her mistake. She stared from Ischian to Pharaoh's stony countenance. Dropping her hands, she stepped back, her sudden pallor betraying her guilt.

Pharaoh rose and moved between them. He looked at his wife with a cruel intensity which made her shiver, then transferred his gaze to that of the merchant.

'So, you know no one in my court?' he said at last, then as he received no answer, he signalled to the captain to approach.

'Take this man and the slave Merya to the guard room. Nefren, accompany the Lady Serana to her apartments. See that she remains there. Set a guard to see that my orders are obeyed.'

Serana stirred herself to action. 'Lord,' she said quietly, you wrong us all. I knew this man a long time ago. I swear that his visit here is with completely innocent intentions. I beg you to re-lease him. Merya knows nothing.'

'She was seen with him yesterday in Thebes.' His answer was cold. 'If she is as innocent as you would have us believe, her interrogation will prove the fact. Please do what I ask and go with

Nefren. Remove the girl, Captain. I will follow in one moment.'

Serana allowed herself to be propelled from the room by Nefren and Pharaoh turned to face Ischian.

'You love my wife.' The accusation was bald.

Ischian nodded. 'I worship her, but she is guilty of no infidelity. I came only to see her, nothing else.'

'It was to you that she came on her escape from the palace?'

'Yes, I offered her honourable marriage but she was with child.'

'You ask me to believe that she was pure during the weeks of the journey?'

'By my god, I swear it.'

Pharaoh smiled. 'We will see if you will still swear it when my guards have completed their work. Take him away.'

Captain Men-ophar fastened Merya to a horizontal bar between two pillars. Merya shuddered as she thought of its obvious purpose. The captain was a merciful man. He disliked hurting women and he came round to face her, his kindly face grave.

'You must tell the truth child, everything you know, and at once.'

'Correct, Captain.' Pharaoh moved him gently out of the way and smiled down at the terrified girl. 'I am sure Merya means to be sensible. She is well aware of *some* of the things that will happen to her if she is not. If she answers my questions satisfactorily, she has nothing to fear — yet.' The pause before the final word gave it its ominous ring and Merya swallowed and moistened her dry lips. She was too frightened to scream or even plead for mercy. She knew, in any case, that it would be useless. She waited helplessly for him to begin.

'You were seen with this man yesterday in Thebes. Do you deny it?'

She shook her head. Her mouth was so dry, she could hardly force herself to answer. 'No, lord.'

'How many times have you met this man?'

'Twice, the day before that, he spoke to me in the street. I had never seen him before. I swear it.'

'He told you he was the lover of your mistress.'

'No, lord.'

'You lie.' He struck her hard across the face, so that her head jerked back with a snap. 'He has confessed freely that he loved my wife. He paid you to help him find a way into the palace.'

The sudden pain had brought tears to her eyes. 'No,' she sobbed, 'it wasn't like that.'

'Explain to me, Merya, just how it was.'

'He wanted to see her, that was all. I told her and she refused. She said it was too dangerous. She told me to bid him return to his own people. My lord, she never thought to be unfaithful, I know she did not. She is innocent.'

Pharaoh drew back and folded his arms. 'Yet

he is here in the palace and by your connivance. Admit it.'

'I suggested that he sold perfumes but my lady knew nothing of the plan. I knew she would be angry.'

'Angry, when she had told you of her love for him.'

'No, no, lord — it was not so.'

'She denied that she loved him?'

'Yes — no — she said . . . please,' Merya broke down and sobbed, 'she said she was afraid for him, that she could never hope to see him again . . . please you must believe me.'

'Unfortunately, Merya, I do not. I wish to know how she planned to meet with this man and what they intended and I want to know in detail and I want to know it quickly.'

'My lord, they made no plans. It was not like that. She said everything was over between them.'

He stepped back and signalled to the waiting official. 'Captain, refresh Merya's memory for me,' he said coldly.

It was much worse than she had imagined. Pain tore through her like a white hot flame. In spite of her determination to remain silent, she heard herself screaming as though from a distance. When it ceased, her head fell forward and she whimpered for water.

'When you have told me what I want to know.' The harsh voice of Pharaoh broke through the pain and she lifted her head, her eyes mutely pleading for him to believe her.

'There is nothing more, lord, I swear it . . . I cannot tell you anything.'

He signalled once more and turned his back.

'No, please,' she cried out beseechingly as Captain Men-ophar once more uncurled his whip and stepped into position.

How long that session lasted she would never know. Her thirst was an agony. When the blows ceased, she was content to hang limp in her bonds and let her body, arched with pain, rest for a moment, but it was only a moment.

Pharaoh lifted her chin and looked fiercely into her eyes. 'Well Merya?'

'By Ma-at, lord, I swear I tell the truth. I can tell you nothing more. You must not harm my lady. She is true to you. Captain, make him believe me.'

The captain spoke quietly. 'Lord, it is possible she speaks true. If she had known any more she would reveal it, I am sure. She is but a child, not a hardened warrior. I feel she has suffered enough.' Never before had he seen his master in this merciless mood. He seemed more devil than man.

Pharaoh regarded the girl's limp body dispassionately. 'Let her down,' he said at last, 'try the man, but I want him alive in the morning. I will see if I have any more success with her mistress.'

Serana appeared outwardly calm when he entered her apartment. One glance at his set face and his fierce command, 'Leave us,' sent the rest of her women scurrying away. He stood with his back against the door, arms folded. She had risen respectfully at his entrance and she made no effort to move.

'You appear to have a loyal maid, madam,' he said coldly, 'in spite of intense pain, she continues to protest your innocence.'

She closed her eyes momentarily, 'Dear God, what have you done to Merya!'

His eyes did not even blink away from their fixed gaze. 'I thought perhaps you might save her further pain by telling me yourself of your shame.'

'Shame!' Anger for a while cast all fear from her and her pale face flushed red with fury. 'What shame should I feel but that which you have caused me to bear? The dishonour that is mine I gained in your harem, when you took me, I who was his betrothed wife. What do I owe you? Have I not given you enough? No, my lord, today I do not intend to cringe before you and beg forgiveness. You have nothing to forgive. That Ischian came to speak to me was foolish, but it shows the true love he bears me — yes, even now. He knew what he risked and will die gladly for my sake. My only regret is for Merya, who only sought to give me pleasure. I know you well enough to realise that we are all doomed to die. At least let her die in peace.'

'You seem very calm, madam, almost brave for the first time since I have known you. Have you any conception of *how* you will die?'

She drew back from him, alarmed by the cold intensity of his fury. 'You are a devil,' she whispered. 'What can you gain by the torture of helpless women?'

'I have treated you with kindness and consideration, hoping in time your coldness and fear of me would dissolve and you would learn to find happiness in my arms. Perhaps I was wrong. Perhaps it was not consideration you craved.'

'I have lain with no man but you. Do you deny that is your son who sleeps there?'

His head jerked up abruptly and she plunged on. 'It is ironic when I think it is not because I do *not* love you, that I and Merya and Ischian must die, but because I *do*. Would I have returned to you when Ischian offered me honourable marriage? If I had not returned he would not have come to search for me and . . . and . . .' she turned from him and stumbled towards the bed, 'I cannot bear to think what he is suffering now. I love him, yes — if that is what you want me to say — but not the way you mean. I love him as I love Raban and Ptah Hoten.' Her head was thrown forward on to the cushion and only muffled sounds came to him from her prostrate form. His hands dropped slowly to his sides and a perplexed expression crept into his fierce eyes. He came forward and took her into his arms. She struggled for a moment as if with her puny strength she would throw him off but he held her arms flat to her body as he turned her to face him and holding her still, forced her against his hard body. He tilted up her face till her tear-filled eyes looked into his own.

'What did you say?' he whispered hoarsely.

She shook her head attempting to blink back the tears but he shook her demandingly, 'Say it — let me hear it.'

'I love you. You have forced me to love you. I belong to you. I should have known it when I made the decision to return but I thought it was because of the child. I know now, when I am most afraid of you, that I shall go to my death loving you.'

He waited for no more. All the pent-up emotion of the last hour was released as his hungry mouth closed on hers and his intense longing was spent in the ecstasy of holding her in his arms.

When at last he released her, he shakily put up a hand to his forehead. 'You are too much for me, little one,' he said huskily, 'it is long since anyone unloosed the demon in me. The gods know I thought it would never again be unleashed, but the thought of you in another man's arms . . . Rest here for a while. I will send the girl to you for tending. Do not fear, I am myself again.'

She caught his hands to delay him for a moment. 'My lord,' she said softly, 'will you not tell me you trust me?'

'Trust you,' he gave her a little crooked smile. 'You know nothing of men, my love. I worship you, but I shall not let you out of my sight for a moment. Do you think I would have behaved as I have today for any other woman in my household? I would have had all three of you quietly strangled. That would have been all. Poor Merya, unfortunate for her, that she has angered me in this way. Do not think I shall not behave exactly in the same way if I feel you ever give me cause again for jealousy. As for your desert lover — I cannot decide even now what to do with him. No . . .' he placed a finger lightly on her lips, 'do not ask me, not just yet. Perhaps tomorrow, after you have shown me how you truly love me and I have shown you what you have never known, the pleasure and delight I am skilled enough to give you, then ask me again and perhaps I will listen. Now kiss me once and lightly, or I shall never be able to leave you and that would prove hard for the two in the guard room.'

# 20

Ahmed sped like an arrow from the bow through the gardens until he could hide himself behind some bushes and watch the outside door of the guard house. His heart thudded within his breast and he brushed away the scalding tears which threatened to blind him. Stupid, boastful, cowardly dolt that he was, he had betrayed Merya who had been like a sister to him. For almost an hour he remained crouched like an animal, then stealthily he approached the guard room itself. There seemed no sign of Pharaoh, so he knocked on the door, then pushed it slowly open.

The captain looked surprised at his entry but as he made no attempt to forbid him access, he came in and closed the door.

'Ahmed, why are you here? I thought you had seen enough of this place.'

'I wanted to know about the slave girl Merya. What will they do to her?'

The captain shook his head gravely. 'If you are fond of the girl, I am sorry. By her connivance a man entered the women's quarters to meet illicitly with the royal wife. For this she must die.'

'Can nothing save her? She is so young — and the man?'

'He too,' the captain shrugged. 'They both knew the risk. It is *how* they will die that saddens me.'

'Almost certainly it will be impalement,' the other guard said, taking a swig of barley beer, 'otherwise he would have ordered an immediate execution and his command was to keep both of them alive.'

Ahmed went faint with horror. He knew full well what the sentence would mean; a slow lingering death lasting perhaps days while the tortured body wriggled on a sharpened stake. It was terrible enough that it should happen to the man — but to Merya. Such a fate was unthinkable.

Captain Men-ophar took pity on his anguish. 'It is by no means certain that it *will* be so,' he said gently.

The boy lifted tortured eyes to him. 'But you think it possible?'

'The girl chose to meddle with someone of importance to Pharaoh. I have never seen him in such a fury.'

'I must see her, Captain. Unwittingly, I brought her to this.'

'Impossible, lad,' then as he saw the boy's desperate need, he relented. 'For two minutes only — or you will get me a flogging. Come, she is in here. Be careful what you say.'

Merya lay on the lime-stone slab where he too had lain in his pain. He saw her pale wraith-like face loom out of the gloom and stooped to speak to her.

'Can I give her water?'

'Only a little. She is fevered.' The captain shook his head as the boy lifted hers and gently held the jug to her tortured lips. He left the door ajar and returned to the outer room.

'Merya,' Ahmed returned the jug to the floor and stroked back her sweat-streaked hair, 'can you hear me?'

'Yes, Ahmed. You should not have come here.'

'Please listen. What can I do? It was I who betrayed you. Like a fool I gossiped to Nefren. I saw you with the Bedouin but I did not know. I thought him an admirer. You must forgive me.'

'Child, of course I do. You were not to know. Comfort yourself. We both of us knew the risk and took it. My only concern is for my lady. He would not believe me. My death is sure but I may yet have convinced him of her innocence by my silence, if only . . .' she broke down and then forced herself to go on, 'if only they do not hurt me any more . . . until . . . until . . . it is time.'

'Pharaoh may yet reprieve you. You know his rages are sudden, but his changes of mood are just as swift. Take courage, lady.'

'Ahmed, I am not deaf. I heard what was said out there. I know what impalement means.'

Ahmed cradled her in his arms. 'You must not think of it,' he whispered.

When the door was summarily thrust open at

215

Pharaoh's entrance, he was caught there and was too grief-stricken to even be afraid of the consequences.

'Go back to my apartments, Ahmed, and await me there.' Pharaoh's voice was curt.

The boy could do nothing but obey, though he feared the stern face of his master boded no good for the tortured girl.

Pharaoh's voice was cold but surprisingly lacked the note of fury it had previously held.

'You are foolish to arouse the devil in me, Merya. If you ever repeat such an action I fear you will not live to see the next sunrise. As it is, I am afraid you will carry the marks of my displeasure until the day you die. But that day will not be tomorrow. Partly due to your loyalty, your mistress is safe. How bad is your pain?'

'My pain is gone, lord, when you tell me my mistress is in no danger.'

'I will send a priest to tend you. Captain, the Lady Serana requests that the girl should be carried to her apartments. See to it.'

He walked into the outer guard room and signalled for the door to be closed. 'How is the Bedouin?'

'He fainted, my lord, but he says nothing different from the information you heard from the girl. It seems it was a foolish escapade but no crime was intended.'

Pharaoh was thoughtful. 'I have not yet decided what to do with him, but tend his wounds. I will send you my orders in the morning.'

Raban, horrified by snippets of gossip he had heard in the palace, hurried to his sister's apartments. He feared that entrance would be denied him, but was relieved when the guard courteously allowed him inside. He found his sister pale but calm. She rushed to his arms and while he held her close, sobbed out her story.

'Quiet, little sister,' he said at last. 'Tell me, where is Merya now?'

'In the guard room. I fear they have tortured her.'

'Poor child, she was born to cause mischief. You say he has promised to forgive her?'

Serana dried her tears. 'He said he would send her to me for tending.'

'And Ischian?'

'I don't know. He would not commit himself. Raban, I dare not say anything more to him yet.'

'No, of course not. Ischian must take his chance. He was mad to put you in such peril. Sister, you do not love Ischian, you had not thought to try and go with him?'

Serana took his hand and held it tightly. 'I love Pharaoh. I should have known it from the beginning. I hate this life here in the harem — one of his bevy of women — but like them I shall only live now for the moments when he pleases to grant me his favours. I know he will quickly tire of me, but at present he has need of me, and in that lies my happiness. In the future, it will be my comfort.'

He patted her hand in the comforting gesture

she recalled from her childhood. 'May our god give you his love, if that is what you desire, my sister.'

Both were disturbed and shocked by the sight of Merya's suffering. She was placed gently on a couch in a room next to Serana's sleeping chamber and Ptah Hoten came himself and carefully tended the sick girl. He said nothing but Serana sensed his pity. He gave her a draught which would cool any fever and allow her to rest. The lash wounds gave him cause for concern but he dressed them with a thick aromatic salve spread on clean linen and at length, took his departure. Serana sat with the slave girl until she fell into an exhausted doze. Just one question Merya asked her.

'Do you know that he loves you?'

Serana had no need to ask whom she meant. She smiled and nodded. 'Perhaps now that we both know of the other's love, it will be easier,' she said quietly.

The other slaves gave their mistress curious glances while they assisted at her toilet. They had doubted if she would remain their mistress, earlier, when news of the affair had swept the palace. Merya's fate was the subject of shocked gossip. Yet here their mistress was insisting that she look her most beautiful tonight and indeed, far from looking pale and anxious as they had expected, her beauty had been heightened by a dawning radiance, they found it hard to understand. Certain that he would summon her, Serana dressed with care. She chose a robe of softest blue to reflect the colour of her eyes and donned the golden necklace he had given her. Tiny golden ear ornaments, a present from Ashtar, completed her finery and she let down her unusual golden hair and combed it till it shone under the lights from the oil lamps. Not one of the beauties of the harem could boast of such fairness. She was unique.

As the hours passed and Nefren did not appear bearing the expected command, she grew a little restless. She entered the nursery and gazed down at her sleeping son. Only a few hours earlier, she had thought never to see him again. Thank the gods, he slept peacefully through the storm which had threatened his mother's life and would perhaps have bereft him of his father's favour.

As the night wore on, she knew that she would not be sent for to the royal apartments. He had obviously chosen another bedfellow. She allowed her silent attendants to undress her and put her to bed. She dismissed them courteously and as the last lamp was extinguished, she lay perplexed, staring at the ceiling. She could have sworn that he had loved her when he held her in his arms. Why else had he spared her? Yet his summons had not come. As usual the man remained an enigma.

She must have slipped into an uneasy sleep, exhausted by the stress of the day's events, for it was about an hour later that she was awakened by her door quietly being opened. Alarmed, she sat up and peered across the room. She had sent her women away and they would not disobey her by returning.

He came to her side and gently placing his hands upon her shoulders, forced her back against the silken cushions.

'It is I, do not be afraid.'

Relief flooded through her. 'My lord, I had thought you would send for me.'

She felt him slip to his knees by the bed and take her fingers in his own firm ones.

'But tonight, I come as a humble suppliant, not as your master. Is it your wish that I stay?'

She leaned forward to see if he were indeed mocking her, but she could not discern his features in the dimness of the room. In any case, it mattered not. She was content that he should be there. She opened her arms and welcomed him as she had never thought it possible for her to do.

Serana wakened early when the first streaks of light appeared in the sky and were visible from her window. He was asleep still, his body magnificent in repose. She leaned forward in an impulse of tenderness and kissed the chest where the powerful thrust of muscles could be seen moving evenly with the sleeper's breath. He did not stir, so she slipped from the bed, throwing a robe lightly round her and went to the window to see the splendour of Ra's rising.

'Come back to me. Who gave you permission to leave?' his command came from the shadows behind her and she turned, her lips parting in

220

an amused smile.

'Who is now the humble suppliant?'

He pushed himself up on his side, propping his head on his bent arm. 'That was last night. Pharaoh is himself again and no longer under the spell of the enchantress.'

She came back and prostrated herself before him, her forehead touching the ground. 'Your slave hears and humbly obeys, lord.'

He gathered her up and drew her down once more into his arms. She was content to rest there and feel the steady beat of his heart close to her own. If only she could keep him like this, tender and happy, her cup of bliss would be full, but she knew it could not be so. As he had said, Pharaoh was himself again, and would soon be deciding the fate of Ischian. Woman-like, she knew it would be unwise to press him to a decision. The ecstasy she had know in his love-making had stirred her to a passion she had not realised was in her nature. The fear aroused by her previous experience had caused her to freeze even when she had most wanted him to caress her. Tender as a woman, he had accepted her withdrawal and wooed her gently until she knew supreme bliss in his embrace. Together they had become one, and it left both content, without the frustrated exhaustion which often followed such experiences.

He moved suddenly and put her aside. 'My love, I must rise and attend to state affairs. I will make arrangements for our journey to Memphis. We may have to delay several days until Merya is well enough to accompany you. You will wish to take her. Let me know how she is after the priest has seen her again.'

Merya was slightly fevered when she woke. She winced sharply when attempting to move and Serana bade her lie still. She fed the girl herself and averted her eyes when she questioned her anxiously about Ischian.

'I do not know, child. I have had no word yet. Try not to worry. Drink some of this draught the priest left.'

Serana was abstracted while the women chattered. One half of her wished to dwell only on her own happiness, but the other vital part of her being almost shrieked to know of Ischian, even while her mind dreaded to face unwelcome tidings. There was no word from Pharaoh. She knew he would be occupied with the morning audience and there were many plans to be made concerning the ordering of the household for the proposed visit to Memphis. When Pharaoh was at last announced, she stilled her rising dread and rose to meet him.

'Greetings, my wife. I bring you a visitor who wishes to take his departure. I know you will wish him well.'

She checked for a moment at sight of Ischian by his side. He was pale but did not appear unduly weakened by the suffering she knew he had endured the previous day.

'Ischian, I rejoice to see you,' she said evenly.

Ischian looked up at the face of Pharaoh, 'May I touch her hands?'

'Indeed you may. I will even leave you together alone for a short time while I visit my son. He paused in the doorway as he signalled for the attendants to leave them, 'I am sure I can trust you both to be discreet.'

'Ischian, oh my dear, what have they done to you?' with tears in her eyes, Serana took his outstretched hands and pressed them.

'Little indeed. It was nothing — forgotten, now that I have what I came for, I have seen you and I do not ask if you are content. I saw love flame into your eyes at his entrance. I am satisfied.'

'Ischian, I have treated you badly. Forgive me.'

'Fate has dealt us both hard blows. We will survive. I do love you Serana. I desired you the first time I saw you in your father's caravan train and I shall never cease to love you, but you did not return my love then, you only promised that you would try to. That you now love another is my misfortune and fear is like a stab wound to my heart when I think what harm I might have caused you.'

'He is a strange man. I shall never cease to fear him, but he is my only love. Try to understand, Ischian, and be happy. Find a wife among your own people.'

'I will, for my tribe too will need an heir and it is well that he should be my son and not Pharaoh's. He has released me. I leave tonight with a caravan to Midian.'

'You are well enough to travel?'

'Quite well enough. What of the slave girl? Did they hurt her?'

'She is weak from the ordeal of questioning, but will recover.'

Ischian handed her a small leather bag. 'Will you give these gold coins to her. I thought perhaps she would wear them as ornaments as our women do and that she will not think too hardly of me. I asked him to sell her to me, but that he has refused to do.'

'He will not part with what is his.'

Ischian smiled grimly. 'That I see, only too well.' He looked up at Pharaoh's return. 'Would it be possible for me to see your son?'

Serana looked questioningly at her husband. He nodded briefly and she fetched the child and placed him in Ischian's arms.

'He is a fine boy, very like his father. I would have loved you well, little son of Serana, but I see you more clearly leading Pharaoh's chariots into battle, than tending my herds.' He kissed the child as a silent blessing and returned him to his mother's arms.

Her last remembrance of him was a gently regretful smile as he bade her farewell, his hands briefly brushing head, lips and heart in the time-remembered manner of her people.

# 21

Serana could never have imagined such a period of quiet happiness as she experienced on the Nile journey to Memphis.

'I wish you too could find the happiness I have, Raban,' she said quietly to her brother one day when Pharaoh and his Vizier were paying a formal visit to the local Nomarch and they were alone together.

He turned at once. 'It gives me delight to see yours, my sister, why should you think me unhappy?'

'You love Merya, isn't that so?'

He sighed, 'I am afraid so. I thought at first it was only a friendly interest but I confess to finding the minx irresistible.'

'Pharaoh said last night he would be prepared to send Merya to you, if you so desired it.'

Horror showed in his face. 'I would not think of it. If Merya were free I would ask for her in marriage, but I cannot force the girl into a relationship she has no choice but to accept.'

Serana said nothing further. She knew her brother's mind and to obtain Merya's freedom seemed impossible at present. If she were to give

Pharaoh another child, she might have the courage to ask this favour. For the moment, she felt he had given her much.

The whole court was pleased to bask in the joy of Pharaoh's new love. While previously, some pretty slave girl had relieved his boredom for a few days, but as quickly annoyed and irritated him, this serene lovely woman appeared to grant him the solace he needed. He was less touchy and arrogant, though still demanding, but officials felt it less of an ordeal to approach him. In Memphis the state visit was a success. Serana felt the old capital a haunt of decaying grandeur after the more modern and sophisticated Thebes but as she had seen little of Egypt outside the palace walls, everything was a source of delight and interest to her.

Ptah Hoten was delighted to see her well and radiant, on their return. Her delighted little cries on the reunion with her son pleased him and touched Sen-u-ret's gentle heart. All seemed well and she was relieved at last to settle once more into her comfortable apartments in the House of Women.

Pharaoh made his customary visit to the harem, made his escape as soon as possible and went straight to Ashtar's apartments. She greeted him with courtesy, but he detected an odd note of reserve in her manner.

'I do not need to ask you, lord, if you enjoyed the visit,' she said quietly as he installed himself in a comfortable chair and she sat on a stool beside him, 'I hear the Lady Serana is well and in excellent spirits.'

He leaned forward and took her hand, 'I am so happy Ashtar, it is almost unbelievable. She is lovely and intelligent and has enough fear of me to make my possession of her interesting.'

Ashtar laughed, 'Perhaps it was well after all that you took my advice that day.'

'I think she has found happiness, though it seemed when first the child was born that her dread of me would make a permanent barrier between us. And you, my lovely Ashtar, forgive me if I err in taste by mentioning it, but you do not look well.'

'Oh,' she laughed off his concern, 'I am well enough, some temporary upset, do not concern yourself about me, lord.' She rose and moved away from him. A frown creased his brow, it was not like his lovely Ashtar to be restless like this, in his presence. Of all his women, she was the least afraid of him. What worried her now, that she was anxious not to reveal? He decided to be flippant and perhaps her reserve would pass.

'I hope you have been discreet in my absence,' he said teasingly. He was alarmed at the reaction his thoughtlessly uttered words provoked. She went white to the lips and stared at him wordlessly.

He drew her down beside him. 'Ashtar my dear, what is it?' he asked quietly.

She turned her head from him and gazed out

of the window. 'You might as well know it now as later,' she said dully, 'I am almost sure I am with child.'

He was silent and she turned a hopeless face back to him. 'What is the punishment, lord, meeted out to an unfaithful wife? If it must be slow, execute it on me alone. Spare him.'

As he continued to stare at her intently, she impulsively leaned forward and touched his hand. 'Let free your fury, lord — say something. It has never been your way to be cruel with me. I deserve your anger — but speak.'

'You are sure?'

She nodded, 'It is early days yet, but I am sure. The signs are unmistakable.'

'How long?'

'About five weeks, possibly a little longer . . .'

He cut in quickly, 'Have you mentioned this to anyone — anyone at all?'

'No, not even Rehoremheb. I have not seen him since.'

'Then you have no cause for unhappiness. In the fullness of time, you will bear a child to Pharaoh.'

She lifted her head slowly and gazed at him unflinchingly, then she put up her hand to check the sudden tears. 'You would do this — even this, for me?' she said brokenly. 'But it is not possible. All the court knows you have not summoned me for months, not since your son was born.'

'But I shall summon you tonight. What more

natural than on my return. The birth will be premature, but what of that?' He shrugged. 'Who will dare question what Pharaoh accepts as his own.'

'I cannot ask this of you,' she said in a whisper. 'What of Serana? It will grieve her. She will think you reject her.'

'Serana is my wife and she will accept the situation. Indeed she will have no choice.' He stood up, his decision made, unwilling that she should thwart his will.

'You will tell her?'

'Neither of us must tell anyone. If one person suspects, I must put you to death with the shame and ignominy your crime warrants. Only they will not suspect. Swear to me, Ashtar, you will not reveal this even to Rehoremheb. He must think what all Egypt thinks. Do you understand?'

She nodded dumbly and stooping, kissed his sandal thong. He lifted her and tilted up her face. 'Listen now, and then I shall never refer to the matter again. You have no need to thank me now or ever. The debt I owe you can never be repaid. When I was in despair, you gladdened my heart, though your own was close to breaking. I cannot give you happiness, but I can save you from destruction, and that I will. I shall have the delight of welcoming another child into my home, your child. There is but one other way. There are women in Thebes who would rid you of your burden but I do not advise it.'

She shuddered and he touched her shoulder comfortingly.

'Then it is settled. Prepare yourself to please your lord and leave the rest to me.'

Serana was looking her most beautiful and was humming to herself happily when Merya entered her room, later that evening. One look at the girl's grave face caused her to put down the small harp and call the girl to her.

'Something is wrong, Merya. What is it?'

'Nothing, my lady.' The girl forced a smile and picked up the discarded instrument. 'You are making progress but slowly. You hardly played at all on the journey. You must practise more frequently.'

'I had no opportunity. Pharaoh claimed all of my time and attention. Even now I wait for him either to come himself or summon me to his apartments. Do I look my best, Merya?'

Merya eyed her quickly and looked away. 'The robe is very becoming, lady,' she said hurriedly.

'The green suits me I think. It is quite new and has been delivered while we were away. He gave me this new collar when we were in Memphis. The emeralds are magnificent. It is my first opportunity to wear them.'

Merya moved away and mechanically began to straighten the disarranged room, placing the toilet requisites and rejected jewelry in a large inlaid chest by the bed. 'I am sure he will admire the robe, lady.'

'Merya, you are quiet. Something is wrong. Do your wounds pain you again?'

'No, lady, it is not that.' Merya hesitated then

came impulsively to her mistress's side. 'Lady, I would rather you hear the news from me now than the girls' chatter. I do not think he will come tonight.'

'Not come, but why, Merya, is he ill?' Serana rose at once, concern apparent on her lovely face.

'No, lady, not ill, he has summoned his favourite, Ashtar, to his apartment. It is talk all over the women's quarters. He visited her almost as soon as he returned and commanded that she come early to his room.'

Serana went white to the lips and sank down suddenly on her chair. She had prepared herself for the time when his interest would wane, perhaps during pregnancy when her beauty for a time would be impaired or even a new slave acquisition would tempt his jaded palate for the moment, but that this should happen so soon and without warning, was more than she could bear.

'Please, Merya,' she said quietly, 'leave me alone. Tell the other women to stay out of my apartment. I do not wish to see anyone.'

'My lady, do not grieve — he loves you, I know he does. This is but a passing fancy. You must have courage.'

'Merya, I don't wish to discuss it. Please leave me alone. Thank you for telling me. I would not have liked to make a fool of myself before the women, but please go.'

Merya looked at her anxiously, then she bowed and did as she was commanded. Well she knew there was nothing she could say, no comfort she could offer. Serana took the magnificent collar from her throat and raised it to her lips. Its cold splendour spoke to her of him. It echoed his awe inspiring grandeur and had seemed in keeping with the man himself. Unhindered tears splashed down on to the carefully goffered pleating of her robe. She made no attempt to check her sobs. Once she was sure that she would be alone, she threw herself on to the bed, buried her head in the cushions and unmindful of her new finery, gave way to a storm of passionate weeping.

Serana made no reference to Pharaoh's neglect of her the following day or later. As the days passed and he made no visits to her apartments, not even to see his son, she judged she had displeased him in some way that she could not understand. Nefren called each morning for a report on the health and well-being of the little heir, but he brought no message from his master. It seemed that he wished to ignore her very existence.

When he at last came to her apartments one evening about two weeks later, he found her laughing with Merya as their heads were bent over the harp. The final discordant note was still sounding as he bowed to her and spoke respectfully.

'Pharaoh asks that you will grace his apartments with your presence, lady.'

So it had come at last, the summons she had longed to hear over the long days since their last meeting. Perversely, she felt angry now that it was accompanied by no explanation but was merely a bald command that he wanted her and expected her at once to obey.

She looked at Nefren coldly and struck several notes on the harp on her knee. 'Thank your master, but tell him I would prefer to decline the invitation.'

Nefren's eyes opened wide. He choked. 'Lady,' he said quietly, 'you cannot wish me to take such a message to Pharaoh.'

'I care not what you tell him, Nefren. It matters not. The import is the same. I shall not go.'

'I beg of you to consider.'

She stood up facing him and threw back her head proudly. 'I have considered, considered well. I have had plenty of time to do so over the last few days.'

'Lady, I must tell you that such an answer will anger him, and wife or not, he could order you punished.'

'Nefren, you know well it will not be the first time, or I imagine, the last. I will not change my answer. I am not one of the slaves who gladly crawl to his presence. Bid him summon one of them.'

'You are determined? You know what it might cost?'

'Very well. Take him my message. I will answer for its meaning.'

He could do nothing but obey. Outside the royal apartment he paused and took time to consider.

'The Lady Serana is indisposed, lord,' he rephrased her message with the lie he hoped would not be held against him in the day when his heart should be judged against the feather of truth in the Hall of Judgement. 'She begs that you will excuse her.'

Pharaoh slowly lifted his head and stared at him. 'You believe her?' he questioned harshly.

'My lord,' Nefren shrugged his shoulders helplessly, 'I have only her word.'

'By Ammon, she has courage. I will grant her that. How dare she disobey me. Indisposed indeed! You will take a carrying chair and go accompanied by my guard. Tell her Pharaoh brooks no refusal. If she is ill, we will send for a healer priest.'

Nefren's embarrassment was evident when he once more presented himself before Serana. She waited calmly for him to speak.

'Lady, I have outside a carrying chair. I have express orders from Pharaoh to take you to his apartments. If you refuse to enter it, I must order the guard to carry you.'

Merya jumped up and, startled, threw out a hand to take her mistress's own.

'I see.' Not a muscle of Serana's face moved. 'I understand. Forgive me, Nefren, that I caused you distress. I see that I must accompany you and give my answer in person. You may dismiss the guard and I shall not need the chair. I will come with you without force.'

'Lady,' he sought to detain her as she moved

to walk past him into the corridor, 'I beg of you, for your own sake, to be sensible. He can be terrible in his rage.'

She paused and looked steadily back at him. 'I understand. Please do not concern yourself about me, nor you, Merya. Await my return.'

She swept into his room and stood, making no obeisance, though she waited until she was addressed.

'I see you have recovered, madam,' he said mildly, without rising from his seat.

'I was never ill, lord. I think Nefren misconstrued my message. I said I was unwilling.'

He did not lose his temper but his lip curled. 'Aren't you being a little childish? You know full well that a request from me amounts to a command.'

'I am your wife, or so I understood, not your slave. There are many beauties in your harem. I am sure any one of them would be honoured by your — request.' She stressed the word deliberately, determined to make him show anger.

He refused to rise to her bait, but leaned back in the chair, his hands linked behind his head, his gaze travelling over the length of her slim tense body. He knew she was afraid, though none would have guessed it. Her blue eyes blazed with anger and her mouth was held in a thin line, her chin pointed upwards in defiance. He was amused but piqued at her determination to bring dire punishment on her own head. She seemed almost anxious to court it.

'You are my property,' he reminded her quietly. 'Once before, I think, I showed you that I demand obedience to my will. Have you so quickly forgotten or must I teach you again?'

'If it is your wish to treat me as a slave, it were better that you sold me in the common market. My position would then be plain for all to see. At the moment I was under the impression that my place as your wife entitled me to some consideration at your hands.' Her hands were clammy with sweat. The very sight of him brought her a bitter sense of delight. Despite her own innermost warnings she felt impelled to goad him to anger.

He smiled broadly and coming over to her, ran his hands from her shoulders over her firm high breasts to her waist. 'I do not think you would really enjoy being exhibited in the market, though doubtless you would at this moment fetch a high price. Never have I seen you so lovely.'

She drew back from his touch and he placed an iron hand round her waist in a sudden sharp movement, crushing her body hard against his own. 'As for your contention that I show you no consideration, am I not merely demanding my rights as your husband? Even your desert lover would have expected you to perform your wifely duties. Am I to expect less of you?'

'Ischian would not have expected me to share his favours.'

'Ah, there the trouble lies.'

She could have bitten out her tongue rather

than appear like his quarrelling women who complained petulantly of his neglect of them.

'But Ischian is not Pharaoh. I have the power to command any woman in Egypt to give herself to me, willingly or unwillingly. Come, my wife, have the hours spent in my arms been so unpleasant? I had not supposed you so unwilling to respond.'

She tried to free herself and sulkily turned away. 'I am not in the mood.'

'Indeed,' she felt his mood change as his tone hardened, 'come now Serana, no more nonsense, must I force you or will you behave sensibly?'

She longed to capitulate and let his caressing hands woo her to respond to his skilful love-making, but she could not give in. He had hurt her too deeply by his belief that he only had to beckon and she would return like a tame animal to his side. She struggled once more, but his grip was like iron and she beat puny fists against his chest, crying like a child in helpless frustration and anger. Her light blows seemed only to amuse him and he swept a demanding mouth upon her own, suffocating her and lifted her effortlessly and conveyed her to the bed.

He took her brutally, savagely and she had thought never to know such pain and blind agony of mind. She cried out to him, pleading for mercy but his passion seemed to leave him bereft of sight and hearing and she could only surrender and endure. When it was over and his anger had spent itself, she lay crying silently, too exhausted to move. Even that first time, when she had been ignorant and afraid, she had never unleashed in him such an animal passion as he had displayed tonight. It was cold comfort to realise that she had brought this punishment on herself by her stupid taunting. The knowledge that this side of him existed was a revelation. She knew now that in all his dealings with her, he had spared her much. Now, by her own foolishness, she had tasted what his anger could mean and she knew it was only a beginning. If she continued to defy him, she knew what to expect.

He sat up abruptly and gazed down at her. A half tender smile played about his mouth and he placed a light finger to her cheek and trapped a slow tear.

'I told you once, little one, never to draw out the demon in me. You gave no heed to my warnings. Why must you be so foolish? Ashtar did not treat me to a display of childish temper because I chose to take you with me to Memphis.'

Fury made her lash back at him. 'Ashtar does not love you . . . I . . .'

He checked her with a kiss, tender and gentle this time, and drew her taut body into his arms. 'So my little one is jealous?'

'Why should not I show anger when I know you are in another's arms? Were you not furious when you thought of me with Ischian?' She was not completely cowed and she drew away and stared demandingly down at him.

His answer was teasing. 'It is a man's right

to demand fidelity from his women. It is the law of life. I am satisfied as to your reasons. Nevertheless, these childish tantrums must stop. I cannot allow you to provoke me before my personal attendants. I warn you if this happens again, I shall be forced to make a public example of you and order you whipped. Every Egyptian husband is allowed to discipline his wife. It is the law, and indeed customary. I am certainly no exception.'

'*Order* me whipped?' her shocked whisper amused him.

'You know well enough I will allow no man to lay hands on you but myself, but it will save you nothing, for I shall not spare you, though you are indeed the love of my life and my heart's joy.'

She gazed wonderingly at him. 'And Ashtar?'

He kissed her forehead where her hair grew low and drew her head to his shoulder. 'I have a deep affection for Ashtar but she knows well where my heart lies and so, I think, do you.'

Serana drew a deep breath and curled up in his arms, content. In the morning she would feel the bruises of his rough handling, but tonight, she felt nothing but the delight of being safe at his side. He had not rejected her. He needed her still and the knowledge that she could arouse such a storm of fury, told her that her possession of this part of him still held firm. She could never lay claim to all of the man. There would be times when she would have to share him and eat out her soul in bitter anguish, but when he once more was prepared to turn to her, her joy would be boundless. For the present, that was enough.

# 22

When Serana knew that Ashtar was to bear Pharaoh a child she forced herself to rejoice in her friend's happiness. She at once sent to congratulate her on the favour of the gods.

One afternoon, they sat together in Ashtar's apartment. Serana was anxious about Pharaoh, who had taken a detachment of cavalry to deal with a disturbance in the north on the borders of Punt.

Ashtar watched her closely and knew her friend was afraid for his safety. 'He has been to war before, you know,' she said gently, 'he will return safely enough.'

'Oh, Ashtar, if he should be caught by a stray spear even, it is always possible.'

'He is well guarded and is a fine commander. I do not fear for him. They tell me the rising is of little account. He will easily put it down, take a few slaves, put to death the rebels and return in a few days. He has survived many years of power. I think Egypt is content with its Pharaoh. You worry unnecessarily, though indeed, I know how you feel. I have been through all the pangs myself.' She paused and looked intently at her friend. 'You must be very jealous of me, Serana, now he is your whole life.'

Serana came impulsively forward and knelt at Ashtar's side. 'Do not think of it. I am ashamed that I envied you even part of his favour.'

'I heard you had quarrelled. Is it true?'

Serana bowed her head. 'It was nothing. I behaved like a spoilt child. No wonder he was furious.'

Ashtar lifted her chin, 'He punished you?'

'As I deserved. I tell you it was nothing. It is all over. I shall not anger him so again. I have learned my lesson. I do not fear pain, only that disgust at my behaviour will drive him from my side permanently. There will be no more tantrums.'

'This was because he sent for me?'

'No . . . well yes, it was. It hurt me that he made no effort to explain. It is ridiculous. After all why should he, he is Pharaoh and I am only one of his women.'

Ashtar dropped her voice, 'I could give you an explanation.'

'Ashtar, you do not have to. I have grown up at last, I can understand.'

The other woman shook her head. 'But you do *not* understand. It is very simple. I am with child. If it were discovered that my lover was the father, I would be put to death and horribly.'

Serana gazed up at her blankly, horror dawning in her great eyes. 'Ashtar, *he* knows?'

'He knows and in the greatness of the man,

he thought only of protecting me, nothing of his own happiness.'

'Oh, Ashtar,' a sudden flood of tears made Serana's voice husky, 'Oh, my dear — do not say another word. To breathe the truth is dangerous.'

'Tell me that you believe me.'

Serana nodded and catching the other's hands bore them to her lips. 'You should not have told me, even to spare me pain. It is dangerous, I see now why he would not whisper, even to me . . . Does Rehoremheb know?'

'Pharaoh has forbidden me to speak of it to anyone. It impinges on his honour. You must give me your word you will not tell him that you know. He would be terribly angry with me. It was just that I could not bear to see you unhappy.'

Serana spoke gently, 'I will never speak of the matter again. Your safety is all that is important now.'

'And that of my child. When I first knew, I was fiercely glad. I wanted so much to bear Rehoremheb's child, then I knew the horror of my situation and my only thought was to survive to bring forth the child. *He* has made that possible. There is none like him, Serana. You are fortunate, for you have his love.'

Serana carried her happiness in her heart like a flame. It was difficult to hide it from those she loved yet she knew it was necessary, for if she were not circumspect, Ashtar would die. Now she longed for the moment when she would see Ashtar's child, for she could welcome it in all sincerity. When Pharaoh returned victorious from Punt, she set herself to give him no sign that she knew his secret. He seemed grave and distant. He embraced her warmly but she sensed he had no joy in his triumph. One of the ring-leaders in the revolt had been a former companion in the School of Youth, where the young princes had been trained, and his betrayal had been a bitter blow. Even more terrible was it, to condemn him to a slow and dreadful death as he was compelled to, as a public reminder to other offenders what the consequences of treachery were.

Ashtar's labour began early and Serana was not surprised. The royal birth chair was sent to the favourite's apartments and the midwife took charge. Pharaoh was informed that it would be some hours before any news could be given, and visited her briefly, and on being told that all was going well, returned to his own apartments.

Serana was content to leave her friend in the capable hands of the temple healers and insisted for once in taking charge of her own nursery. A new nurse was now in charge, a stern woman, Mem-net, who had served as nurse in several noble families but Mern-ptah was now acquiring a mind of his own and resembled his royal father in a firm determination to get his own way. He was a sturdy well favoured child of almost a year, and Serana's heart swelled with pride as she lifted him into her arms. He reached out demandingly for the amulet round Merya's throat and she dangled it in front of his face. He adored the young slave girl and made wild gurgles and noises to indicate his desires. He would soon try his first words.

'You will have to share your father's love, my lad,' she said tenderly, 'you will soon have a new little half brother or sister.'

'Let us pray the gods it will be a sister,' Merya said teasingly, holding the amulet away from his clutching fingers, 'for the succession will then be assured.'

Serana sighed. If it were indeed so, she found it in her heart to pity the mite whose fate would be decided the moment she drew breath. She looked affectionately at her son who grabbed at the charm with regal possessiveness. 'She will have a demanding husband,' she thought.

Merya was inclined to chatter. The women were saying that the birth was very early and it was hoped that the child would live. Serana sharply reminded her that Mern-ptah himself had been prematurely born and had survived to grow strong and healthy. There could be little danger for Ashtar's child.

Late in the evening Ptah Hoten summoned Pharaoh and Serana to Ashtar's apartments. One glance at his face told Serana that all was not well. He wasted no time.

'My lord, the gods have favoured you with the gift of a daughter, but the mother will die before sunrise.'

'I do not understand. The midwife told me the birth was going well.'

The priest nodded. 'The child was born normally. We expected no complications but she has haemorrhaged badly. I cannot save her. It is the will of the gods.'

'But why?' Serana turned tortured eyes in his direction. 'What has caused this — she is young and was strong — I cannot see why this should happen.'

'I regret, lady, I do not know the reason. It baffles me. It sometimes occurs without warning, and there is no treatment that can be successfully administered. If the patient loses so much blood, death is inevitable. It can only be a matter of hours. It was not an unnaturally difficult birth. The child is healthy and well favoured.'

'Does she know?' Pharaoh asked quietly.

'I think she does. She has asked for you.'

Ashtar still appeared her beautiful self as she lay back upon the pillows, except for the unusual deathly pallor of her features. She was not in pain, but seemed simply very tired like a child who desires to sleep after hard play. There were no marks of suffering on her lovely features. Even her luminous dark eyes were not marred by heavy shadows. It seemed unthinkable to Serana that this supremely beautiful creature would soon be no more. The child lay in the crook of her arm and she was smiling tenderly at their approach.

'They told you?' she said softly.

'Ashtar,' Serana's voice was choked with sobs,

'it cannot be true.'

'Little one,' Ashtar's hand came out and touched the shining hair of the kneeling girl, 'you must not grieve so. I trust you to care for my little one. You will do that for me, for in spite of the fact that I am not so old, I have almost regarded you as my daughter and have loved you well.'

'She will be mine from this moment on. I swear,' Serana said quietly and made an effort to blink back her tears as she took the child from her mother.

'It is well,' Ashtar smiled and looked up at Pharaoh. 'She knows. I told her months ago. I know it was a breach of faith but I could not bear to see her unhappiness.' She spoke gently to Serana. 'Will you be jealous if I ask for some last minutes with him alone?'

Serana could not speak. She kissed the lovely brow and Ashtar raised herself to embrace her. 'Wait for him. He will need your comfort, for I think he will miss me, a little.'

When they were alone he knelt down and took her hand, waiting for her to speak.

'Even now it has not been granted that I bear you a son. I longed for it so long. I am fated to disappoint you, lord.'

'My lovely Ashtar. You have done better than that. You have given me a throne princess.'

Her eyes widened and he nodded smiling, 'All is well, fear not.'

She lay quiet for a moment then she said, 'Tell

him what you think best. He knows well how I love him . . . he will be safe, you promise?'

'Give your heart peace.'

'Though I have clung to my childhood's goddess Astarte, I am glad that I shall be buried with the rites of Egypt. Ptah Hoten . . . ?'

'He will go with you. Do not fear. Do you wish me to call him?'

She shook her head. 'Not just yet. Dear lord, hold me once more in your arms. Hold me tight and lie to me that I am as beautiful as ever.'

He drew her tenderly into his arms and her fingers reached up and touched his cheekbones and lips, 'I have loved you well, my lord, though it was not with the whole of my heart's passion.'

'You are dear to me, beloved sister.' She smiled at his words. It had always seemed inappropriate to her of Syrian stock that these Egyptians should speak so of their lovers. It was not so in her own land. Then he felt her tremble and caught her chilled fingers. 'You have nothing to fear, Ashtar. Ptah Hoten will not leave you until you are safe.'

She nodded and indicated that she was ready for the priest's ministrations.

Ptah Hoten drew him gently from the room and prepared to lie down on a couch near her. He spoke comfortingly and under the spell of his insistence, her eyes closed obediently and she slept.

Serana clutched at Pharaoh's arm as he withdrew from the apartment, his face a mask of grief.

'What will he do?' she questioned, frightened.

'He will go with her.'

'But she is dying.'

'That is so,' he nodded, 'he will lie beside her and his Ka will leave his body. He will accompany her to the other side and return when all is well with her.'

Her eyes widened in astonished bewilderment, 'You mean that he will die?'

'It is hoped that he will not. A trained priest should be able to safely accomplish this and return to his body.'

'But there is sometimes a risk?' her question was insistent, and he turned away and was silent for a moment then he turned back to face her.

'There is. It is the risk an initiate priest is forced to take,' he replied, deliberately.

# 23

Ashtar was laid to rest in a rock tomb in the royal valley on the western side of the river. For the customary seventy days, after the embalmers had completed their work, her body was steeped in natron and laid in a mortuary chapel in the Temple of Ptah until the funeral. Pharaoh chose for her a tomb near to that of his own mother and spent most of the time choosing elaborate funeral furnishings and costly gifts to accompany his favourite to the tomb.

Serana's feeling of sadness was accompanied by a strange comfort when she stood beside him in the burial chamber after descending the ramp and passing down the long corridor which connected it and its ante-chamber to the rock entrance. The little room seemed almost a replica of Ashtar's own lovely apartment. The paintings on the walls were bright and gay, reminders of the vivacity and brilliance of the woman herself. Fine furniture, an array of costly linens and silks in chests and jewelry were grouped near the beautiful bed of sandalwood inlaid with ivory. Tears threatened to blind her as she looked at the wonderful collection of perfume jars and toilet requisites placed on a table near the sarcophagus itself. The inner coffin was painted and overlaid with gold leaf. All round her, Ashtar had her most treasured possessions and also thousands of heaped flowers. The scent of lilies and jasmine was almost overpowering in the little room. The priest put down the food offerings and wine jars. All had been done to secure her comfort in the afterworld. Ptah Hoten aided by the priests of the necropolis, had performed the rites which would guide her ankh to its resting place.

Pharaoh spoke just once. 'Good bye, my Ashtar. Sleep well until we, who are all linked by love, come to join you.' Then he left her and when she was quite alone, the tomb was sealed.

Serana was sitting quietly with Merya when Pharaoh came to her apartment that evening. The slave girl prostrated herself and withdrew. Serana had seen little of him during the days of mourning, now she rose and fetched him wine and food. He declined to eat and invited her to sit beside him. She longed to find words to comfort him, but because of the power of the man himself, she felt helpless. It was impossible even to reach out and touch him until he gave her leave.

'I have put the child in our nursery with Mernptah,' she said quietly. 'It seemed best that they should be together. Lord, you seem more than normally distressed. Is there anything I can do to help?'

'No, it is not that we have lost Ashtar, that is terrible enough, but that I was incapable of helping her. This I cannot bear to remember.'

'But you could do nothing. Ptah Hoten said nothing could save her. You must not reproach yourself.'

'Had I been an initiate priest, as I should have been, I could have done for her, what he was able to do.'

She drew back, her face grave, 'But you are Pharaoh. Is this not enough?'

'Pharaoh should be both priest and king. In this I fail my people. I have known it for long, but felt its full pain when Ashtar died. I know in my own heart that I should be initiated, but I am afraid.' It was out and he smiled at her thinly, then turned away as her troubled eyes regarded him intently.

'Of what are you afraid, my lord?'

'Of death,' the reply was low, hardly audible, 'What all mortal man fears.'

'But all men fear death, as you say — you are but mortal.'

He shook his head. 'No, I am son of the gods.' He smiled and she felt there was no answer. 'I know what you are thinking, that my divinity is but a term, a political lie to give me complete control of my people. You are right in part. My divinity is a symbol of the truth that lies in all men, half god — half animal, that is man. It is the mission of the priest to lift the animal-man to the god-man and make him aware of that part of him alone which is real and enduring. To do that, he must not be afraid to put aside the animal body, and quite simply . . . I am so afraid.'

Serana stood up and standing behind his chair, placed her hands on his shoulders, 'This is to be expected. I love this animal man and I too would fear if you decide to endanger it. Do not frighten me, we have only just found each other.'

He turned and smiled, 'We will not talk of it. Come and sit down near to me. We must put grief aside for a while. I have so few opportunities to see you and there is so little I really know about you.'

'You know everything about me that matters. I love you and no other.'

'I have never asked you who engineered your escape from the women's quarters and I will not do so now. I have my own suspicions, but that does not matter. Tell me what made you decide to return. Was it when you first knew about the child?'

'No, Ischian promised to care for me and at first, I wanted to go with him. All was arranged. I was to be his bride.'

'Then what drew you back?'

She sighed, 'I don't really know. I think it was the necklace.'

'Necklace?'

'Yes, you will not remember. After that . . . second time, you sent me a necklace. It was very fine, gold, studded with turquoise. I was very angry at first and did not wish to take it but I thought it might be useful and in any case I could not refuse. I unwrapped it in Ischian's tent and

253

I knew I could not stay. I thought it was because of the child, but I know now it was an excuse I made to myself. Ischian would have loved the child. He would not have been Pharaoh — but he would have grown up strong and happy, perhaps happier than he will be as Prince of The Two Lands. No, it was not my child, it was the thought that I could not shut you out of my mind. You drew me like one of those strange stones which draw articles to them. I didn't want to come back. I couldn't help myself.'

'And the necklace?'

'I gave it to the caravan leader who brought me back to Egypt. His wife was very kind to me.'

'But that was several months before you found Ptah Hoten. What did you do in the meantime? Why did you not come to the palace?'

She laughed, 'Oh, my lord, you talk foolishly. I was an escaped slave. I was terrified. I found work. It was not so very bad, I worked in a tavern first and the owner seemed to like me but his wife was jealous and she cast me out. Then I found work in a vineyard. It was hard because I was heavy with child, but I had to keep us both alive.'

He took her face between his hands and stared fiercely into her eyes. 'I think you have made light of the bad time. I hope the people were good to you.'

She shrugged, 'I was poor and of little account. I cannot complain.'

He released her and smiled grimly, 'I blame myself. Had I treated you more gently, you would not have been so afraid.'

'Perhaps I would not have loved you so well.'

He sighed. 'At least you know the best and the worst in me.' He stiffened and she caught his gaze, which had travelled to the open aperture which led to the garden.

'What is it?' she said quickly.

'Where are your women?'

'On their sleeping mats I imagine. I had dismissed them all but Merya.'

'Who is in the nursery?'

'Mem-net. She sleeps with the children and there is a young Nubian slave girl, but she is little more than a child.'

He relaxed, 'I thought I heard someone in the garden, and as this part of it is private for your use, I was puzzled. It might have been a cat. The gardener's boy has one.'

'Yes indeed. She is to have young. Do you think I could have one for my own?'

He laughed, 'A dozen if you wish. I'll arrange it.'

Her answering laugh rang out. 'I doubt if she will oblige you with that number, even for Pharaoh.' She had turned her back on him to take up her comb from the toilet table and when she turned back she froze, eyes widening with horror. He was leaning back in his chair, some light retort framed on his lips to answer her, completely unaware of the man who had crept up behind him.

The oil lamp glittered on his brown hair and touched his grey eyes, now hard as stone. She had never seen Rehoremheb with such an expression before. It kept her chained to the floor, so paralysed with fear that she could not find use of her tongue to cry out a warning. She knew he held a dagger poised for the thrust although she could not see it. Pharaoh looked up at her, and his own eyes looked wary, puzzlement creasing his brow. She tried to scream, then did the only thing possible, threw herself across the room and tried to seize the dagger-hand of the master builder. She was an easy opponent and he lightly thrust her aside with a little animal snarl of rage. She felt the dagger tear down her bared arm and felt no pain but the warm trickle of blood on her skin. She had fallen full length and sobbed as she tried to rise. Her attack, helpless as she was to prevent him striking, had been enough to put Pharaoh on his guard. He turned and closed with his assailant. Rehoremheb was a heavy man but no match in the wrestling ring. Pharaoh had kept himself in training and though unprepared, he was not hindered by the blind anger which bereft the other of his judgement. He wrenched the weapon from his hand and caught him a heavy blow on the jaw which sent him staggering across the room. Before he could recover, Pharaoh had thrown himself on to him and delivered a second blow. Rehoremheb's head cracked back against the elaborately carved foot of the bed and he lay still. Pharaoh rose and staggered to where

Serana crouched half mad with terror.

'My little love,' he whispered huskily, 'hush now, it is all over. Can you stand up?' He lifted her to her feet, his lips tightening at the sight of the blood marring her robe. 'If he has hurt you, I'll watch him die slowly.'

'No, it's nothing, just a scratch,' she sank down on to a stool and he slipped to his knees to examine the wound.

'As you say, it isn't serious.' Stooping, he tore a strip from his own robe and skilfully bound her arm. Her eyes went to the supine man on the floor.

'Have you killed him?' she asked horrified.

'I think not, but his head hit the foot of the bed. He won't move for a while.'

'And you, are you injured at all? Shall I summon help?'

'No, I am perfectly all right. He was no match for me. Let him lie. I don't wish to call the guard.'

Having assured himself that she was shaken more than hurt, he bent over the unconscious man and examined the head wound.

'I think he is just unconscious. I'll try and bring him round. Bring me some water.'

She fetched a ewer from her toilet table and watched as he threw the water over Rehoremheb. There was a sound of spluttering and scrambling and slowly he sat up and watched them warily, blinking away the water from his eyes. The genial good-humoured man she had known seemed to have vanished. His features were haggard and bloated as though he had been drinking heavily and he, who had taken as much care of his appearance as a young maiden before her first banquet, had neglected himself for days. His copper brown hair was unkempt and matted and his chin unshaven. As his eyes met those of Pharaoh, he croaked, 'Well what are you waiting for? Finish it, or are you saving me for later to give you and your court pleasure? Either way it matters little to me. You have killed her, let me go to join her. Perhaps there I will find some semblance of peace.'

Gentled by a wealth of pity for his terrible loss, Serana knelt at his side and wiped his face with a linen kerchief. 'You are mad, Rehoremheb. What are you saying? No one killed Ashtar. I feel for you dreadfully, my friend, for you know I loved her too, but you must pull yourself together.'

'She died bearing his child, or did I mishear it?' he said, gazing fearlessly up at the black eyes above him.

'She died in childbirth. That is true but by no neglect. She had every care. Everything was done to aid her. You must accept the will of the gods, as we all have had to do. Now stand up, man. You shame yourself before the lady.'

Like a sullen schoolboy reluctantanty obeying a master to whom he gave grudging admiration and respect, Rehoremheb stumbled to his feet and stood for a moment regarding the man whom he had attacked, then suddenly he turned from them and going to the wall of the room, leaning his head down, his arms clawing upwards, he sobbed as if his heart would break. Serana made to go to him, but Pharaoh silently gestured her to leave him alone. She had never before heard a grown man give way like that in her whole life. It tore her heart-strings. His agony of grief was too much for him to bear and the worst of it she knew, was that until now, he had been unable to give any sign of it before others. By virtue of his position, he had no right to mourn Pharaoh's favourite. When it was over, he turned and drew a deep sigh.

'I regret I treated you to such a display,' he said stiffly. His behaviour was still so much like a child's that she longed to throw her arms around him and comfort him as she did Mern-ptah when he bumped himself and required the solace of her caresses.

'Now that you are somewhat more yourself, I suggest you sit down and listen,' Pharaoh said grimly. Rehoremheb hesitated for a moment, and then obeyed. There was no more resistance in him. He was beaten and he knew it and he cared not. He had reached the final abyss of despair, and could find no means of escape from it, nor at that point, did he wish to.

'Ashtar is dead,' Pharaoh's words were brutal and Serana winced at his tone, 'you must face the fact and learn to live without her. I knew that you loved her. I have known it for months. I promised her that you would be safe, and somehow I'll see that you are so.'

Rehoremheb stared up at him wonderingly and Pharaoh caught him by the arm. 'Come with me.' He led him into the royal nursery. Mem-net was asleep in the room next to the children, with the door open and the Nubian girl, who spoke little Egyptian, was curled up on a sleeping mat in the corner. Pharaoh gestured to Serana to ensure that they were not interrupted. She peeped in at the sleeping nurse who was snoring noisily then nodded. Pharaoh moved aside from the cradle which held Ashtar's daughter and signalled for Rehoremheb to approach.

The master builder gazed down at the sleeping baby and stooping, touched the tiny cheek with his finger. The baby stirred and opened her eyes, then once more settled herself to slumber.

'It is as well,' Pharaoh said quietly, 'that she resembles her mother. Perhaps you have noticed that she has grey eyes, a colour which neither I nor her mother possesses.'

Rehoremheb jerked up his head, but the other's expression was enigmatic and as silently as they had entered, he ushered them both back into Serana's room. For a moment, nothing was said, then Rehoremheb sank down abruptly and placed his head down on his folded arms on the table. His muffled words came to them.

'She sent me no word.'

'She could not,' Pharaoh's answer was firm. 'It would have been too dangerous. I thought it best that you should never know, but now I have changed my mind. I think you can be trusted. To us, she will be as our own. You need have no fears for her.'

'It was I who killed Ashtar . . .'

'No one killed her. It was her destiny. You must accept this or you will go mad.'

'That you should have done this thing for her . . . knowing what you know . . .'

'I loved her in my fashion and I love you too and I shall cherish this daughter of hers and you will help me. She will thrive and grow beautiful like her mother and you will be there to show her beauty in wall paintings and sculpture and fine buildings. It will be part of her heritage, that and the throne of The Two Lands.'

# 24

Ashtar's daughter was named Asenath. She was a beautiful child and Pharaoh's pride in his two children was shown in his frequent desire to be with them whenever he could. Rehoremheb, he kept within the palace for a while, saying that he wished him to draw out some plans for a new temple he desired to build. It was obvious to both Serana and himself that the young man could only be reclaimed now by work. After a few days he reappeared at court, shaven and oiled and clad in the height of fashion, but there was a suspicion of lingering sorrow round the erstwhile humorous grey eyes and the joyous delight in living seemed to have utterly deserted him. Serana knew that half of his being dwelt in the rock tomb on the opposite river bank while the other half was given in silent worship to the wilful little scrap in the nursery.

Serana did not trust herself to refer to the matter which she had been discussing with Pharaoh on the night they had been interrupted by Rehoremheb's sudden arrival, but he himself unexpectedly spoke of it a few days later, as they walked in the quiet shade of her private garden.

'I have spoken to Ptah Hoten. I shall begin the long period of temple training within a few days.'

She made no answer but looked up at him as if she would read his very soul. He kissed her lightly on the forehead.

'Look not so agitated, my love. My mind is settled. Ptah Hoten is overjoyed and much can happen before the days of my initiation. I only speak of it now because my training will take time and there will be days when I shall see less of you than of late. You will understand?'

She nodded and bending, kissed his bronzed arm, 'We shall be here my lord,' she said quietly, 'your children and I, waiting for you, whenever you have need of us.'

During the months which followed, Serana watched anxiously for signs of stress in her husband. Outwardly he seemed his normal self but there were gradual changes which she could not help noting. Where he had been before a considerate and just ruler though liable to fits of temperamental petulance, he was now even more exacting in his demands that work should be done faultlessly, though his furies became less frequent. There were times when he seemed somewhat withdrawn and thoughtful and she wondered if the hours spent in the careful training of the will and the determination to force the body to obey its master, were causing distress. She never referred to the subject of his training in words, as she knew it was a secret matter between the aspiring priest and his teacher of wisdom, Ptah Hoten.

One other person noticed a gradual change in Pharaoh's attitude. No longer did Nefren find it necessary to fear punishment, but he was more troubled to sense a withdrawal of Pharaoh's need for his services. Nefren had come very close to his master during his years of servitude and he found this slight barrier which appeared to have been erected between them bewildering and hurtful. If anyone had told him that he had affection for Pharaoh, he would have laughed in their faces, yet he knew in his heart that his master's marks of favour had become important to him over the years and if his need for him had now diminished, there would be a vacuum in his life that he would find it difficult to refill.

He was one day summoned to Pharaoh's apartment to find Ptah Hoten about to leave. There was a tight hard line to the set of his master's mouth which had not been present for several months. Obviously the priest had said words which had displeased him, but his manner was polite, almost respectful, when he dismissed him. Nefren stood a little uncertainly, waiting to be given the reason for the summons. Pharaoh appeared hardly to notice him, then turned with one of those lightning movements he knew well, and moved to a small table where he kept his scrolls and plans.

'Nefren, remove your arm bracelet.' The words were almost harshly uttered and a perplexed frown creased the slave's brow but the habit of obedience was strong and he unclasped the heavy silver bracelet from his left fore-arm and held it open in his hand.

'Put it down, on the table.' Still Pharaoh did not turn. Puzzled, Nefren obeyed, fearing he had displeased his master and continued to await further instructions. At last Pharaoh turned and proffered a small scroll of papyrus, obviously but newly penned by his scribe. 'This is in exchange.'

Nefren reached out and took it and the other's lips twitched. 'You seem surprised. Know you not, Nefren, that as that bracelet was the outward symbol of my possession of you, so its removal indicates my renunciation of that property.'

'You intend to sell me?' Shock made Nefren's voice almost shrill.

'Nefren,' the pronunciation of his name was almost wistful, 'do not be a fool, man, the scroll is your manumission. You are free. You may leave me.'

Nefren rocked with the suddenness of the utterance. He gazed down at the papyrus in his hand and then at the band of white skin where the bracelet had rested. His emotional reaction was too great to even speak his gratitude.

He kissed the floor before the feet of Pharaoh and rising hurried from his presence his heart full of an overwhelming sense of joy. He was unaware of the bitter twist to the other's lips at his hasty departure.

Pharaoh sought Serana in the nursery and found

her trying to quieten Asenath who was screaming for attention. He swept up his furious little daughter in his arms laughing at her rage.

As usual, she quietened immediately and at last was coaxed to sleep. Serana surrendered her son into his nurse's care and followed him into the garden.

'What is it?' she said, alarmed by the sorrow she glimpsed round his mouth.

'I cannot hide much from you, little one,' he said ruefully as he took her hand, 'it is nothing. I merely suffer the inevitable pangs which accompany withdrawal from something which has become very dear.'

'I do not understand.'

'It is simple. I have freed Nefren.'

'Oh, my lord, that is a wonderful thing to have done.'

'For Nefren certainly.'

'Did he ask to buy his freedom?'

'No it was my decision. I know that I cannot keep him by my side in captivity. My love for him is too great for that.'

'What did he say?'

'Very little — in fact I cannot recall anything at all. He left me in great haste. Slavery has been a terrible burden to Nefren, almost too great at times for him to bear. Now he has what his heart desires and I must learn to manage without him.'

As Nefren did not present himself at Pharaoh's apartments during the course of the day, Ahmed made shift to prepare for the evening's feast without him. It was being given in honour of two important Syrian dignitaries, then visiting The Two Lands. Nefren arrived and quietly but firmly dismissed him and took charge. Pharaoh made no comment but allowed himself to be bathed, oiled, and ceremonially attired for the occasion. Nefren was his old quiet, efficient self and his master said at last, 'Is it your intention to return to your own people?'

Nefren stopped what he was doing and returned to stand before him, his face shocked. 'Leave your service, my lord? It had not occurred to me.'

Pharaoh dropped his eyes to hide the triumphant glint in them. 'I am pleased to know that our plans seem to be in agreement. My chief steward is old and has been talking recently of retiring from office. It seems a good time for you to train to succeed him. It pleases me well, that you will stay by my side of your own free will.'

'One question, lord — why did you do it? There was no real need.'

Pharaoh hesitated for a moment and averted his face. 'Because it seemed obligatory at this stage to part with what is most dear to my heart. Since I am not called upon to sacrifice members of my family who are my responsibilities, the lot fell on you, who are that man whom I most love and trust.' As he said the last words, he turned and held out both arms and Nefren took his elbows in his own grasp, for the space of one or two moments, then a little embarrassed, drew back.

'My lord,' he said quietly, 'I can find no words to thank you for your gift nor for your words which go to my heart, only I say that you need never fear that that trust which you place in me now, will ever be misplaced.'

Pharaoh's face was grave, 'It may be, my friend, that I shall need to call upon your services in a shorter time than you think.'

One month later Pharaoh summoned Raban and Nefren to his apartment and spoke to them together.

'Tomorrow I go to the Temple of Ptah to try the ordeal and take my first initiation. If I succeed, I shall return clad in my priest's regalia; if I die, I shall lie prematurely in my rock tomb in the Valley of the Kings. To you both I commend the safety of my royal wife and the heirs to the kingdom. If any danger threatens, it will be for the two of you to contrive an escape. I can envisage no treachery. Ptah Hoten is true as Mat-at and so I believe is Men-ophar, my captain of the guard, but to you both I know Serana is dear, I would leave her happiness in your hands. Mern-ptah must be declared Pharaoh and a ceremonial marriage to Asenath immediately accomplished. You understand?'

Neither made answer but bowed briefly.

'Raban, I give into your hands these scrolls. They are the deeds to my ownership of both Merya and Ahmed. I wish neither of them to pass into the hands of another, in the event of my death. I believe that both will wish to remain in the service of the royal wife and the heirs but this will assure them of a freedom of choice. I know you will care for Merya's well being and the smaller scroll will enable you to give her the marriage gift she will most appreciate, the freedom of her father.'

Raban's eyes filled with tears, 'My lord, I have no words to offer you . . . but surely, these precautions are not necessary.'

'I think they are, my friend. I have a foreboding . . . but no . . . we will not think of that.'

He turned. 'To you, Nefren, I leave the responsibility of rulership. Serana will wear the crown until the children are ready to take the crook and flail into their own hands. It will be for you to guide her. My vizier will accept your office. He has so sworn. After tonight I shall pass into the temple for the space of three days. During that time, you will neither see nor hear news of me. It is then that Serana will need the presence and love of you two she holds dear. You swear to me that you will be true to her.'

Again the two nodded. It seemed that words were not needed. Pharaoh smiled and rose. 'It is well. I am content. I will go now to spend my last hours with her who has gladdened my life. I pray the gods I shall return to her side, victorious.'

# 25

Serana lay wakeful in the luxurious bed in her private apartment. Soon Merya would arrive to waken her, and in fact, she had had no rest since he had left her side. Outwardly she had remained calm and businesslike, going about her duties in the women's quarters where he had left her to see that all ran smoothly until his return. The other women had watched her in a curious detached way. She had thrust aside the idea that they were already beginning to set her aside as one to be reckoned with, in the event of his not returning.

He must return today. Her waiting had seemed interminable and her longing for him was a physical ache. Only three nights ago he had slept peacefully with her in his arms. He had not seemed afraid, though he had held her even closer to his heart on parting. She had not gone with him to the temple.

'No, little one. I want you to go into the nursery and you will not see me go,' he had said and she had obeyed him, as she always had done.

Ptah Hoten had not thought it necessary that he should journey to the Great Pyramid for his trials as many of his predecessors had done before him. Less than a mile away in the temple where her son had been born, they would at dawn welcome a new priest or mourn the passing of Pharaoh. He would remain in a rock tomb alone, without sound to penetrate and in complete darkness. During this time, he must meditate and attempt the mastery of his other vehicles of consciousness the Ka, the Ba, and the Ankh itself. Once he could leave and return to his physical body at will, he would be worthy to enter the priesthood, for he would be master of himself as well as ruler of The Two Lands. She knew instinctively that this lesser death could so easily become the greater one, if his will was not true as Ma-at. She had guessed at his fears and suffered because in the dread moment of his need, she was unable to help.

'If only he had gone from me into physical danger,' she had said to the priest, 'if he were wounded or faced capture, I feel that I could bear this waiting, but this is beyond endurance. If he should fail . . .'

'As Osiris he will come triumphant from the tomb and rule The Two Lands as priest and king as it was destined that he should.' The priest's answer was confident.

'Though he said nothing to me, I know that he had a foreboding of death. All his life he has fought the terror. I know it.'

'Yes,' the priest nodded, 'I know it too and I cannot account for it. His conquering of this fear will accomplish his release from the bondage of the flesh. It is possible that his dreams and remembrances of the past have overshadowed his heart and this would account for his dread of the ordeal. He was fully confident, I am sure, and will succeed. You must not fear for him. My thoughts are with him. He is guarded by faithful priests each second of the time. More we can not do. The victory must be won by him alone. He must cross the abyss of his own doubts. This is the greatest ordeal any human can face, I know only too well, but I have no fears for this man.'

Merya's face was strained when she entered the apartment though she passed no comment on what she knew was in her mistress's thoughts. Serana dressed and forced herself to visit the nursery as usual. The sight of the two babies, peacefully asleep, brought tears to her eyes which she hastily dashed aside. It could not be that Mernptah must assume the sonship of Ra before he could even master his own chubby legs and run to his mother.

She refused food and passed into the garden. It was still early yet the sun was warm, but in spite of it, she shivered as she saw a hawk rise suddenly into the air.

'Fear not, lady. The royal hawk does not yet fly to the sun.' She turned hastily and saw Nefren quietly regarding her.

'Nefren . . . he must come . . . he must.'

'He will, lady, I know it.'

'I wish I were sure. I have known his love for such a short time. I thought the gods would not grant me such ecstasy. They cannot now take it so soon away.'

'No, lady, I do not think they will.'

'Egypt needs him, the children do, we all do.' She broke down abruptly. 'I cannot bear it, Nefren, I know I must try, but I cannot . . . if . . . if I am left alone.'

'Lady, have you eaten?'

She shook her head and he said gently, 'Go and sit near to the pool where he loved to swim and I will bring you refreshment. It will help to give you courage and it will give me something to do.'

She sighed. 'If you insist. I promise I will try.' She turned as Ahmed came to the entrance of Pharaoh's apartment. His expression of concern caused her almost to smile in spite of her anxiety.

'Nefren, I have prepared everything for him. He will need to bathe and robe himself afresh. Will you check and see that I have forgotten nothing?'

Nefren nodded and gestured her comfortingly to the seat by the pool.

All in the Great House was ready for the master. Today he must return. All Egypt waited and it seemed that a hush hung over the garden. The pool was still and she sat down on the marble bench and gazed into its cool depths. It seemed to bring quietude to her seething thoughts and she sat on, content to wait for Nefren's return.

When his shadow darkened the pool, she spoke without turning. 'Put the tray down. I will try some in a few moments.' He did not answer or move to obey her and she turned swiftly fearing that he brought ill news.

Even before her gaze reached his face it checked at the sight of the gilded reed sandals, those which had carried the priest safely over the bridge to the gods. She hardly dared to lift her eyes to his face and before she could do so, his arms had enfolded her and held her close. She waited until her tears were checked for he must not see his royal wife showing the marks of cowardice, then she lifted her eyes to the beauty of his proud face.

There seemed little change in him, only round the eyes a little light appeared to play, or perhaps it was merely a trick of the sun, otherwise there seemed no sign of suffering or a conquest of endurance. He did not appear worried even. His mobile beautiful lips were for once tender.

'I can face you now, my love, fearing nothing,' he said quietly, 'it is over. I am not only Pharaoh, but a priest, young in time and experience, but a priest nevertheless.'

'You are early, my lord,' she said tremulously, as he kissed her gently and gazed down into her eyes, 'I hope all is prepared for you, as you have always commanded.'

Nefren stopped short as he advanced with the tray of food, then bowed low. 'Greetings, lord,' he said respectfully, 'I rejoice to see you. Would

274

you wish me to bring extra food here? Ahmed is ready to rerobe you for the morning's ceremonies.'

Pharaoh laughed. 'It seems that all is as usual, as if I have never been absent. Yes, we will take food here, my friend, after I have paid a brief visit to the nursery. Afterwards I will receive you and the vizier and hear from you, your reports. Raban must come and I will give him what he desires.'

Serana smiled, 'Both he and Merya look confidently for your return.'

'Since my death might have granted them greater happiness, that is a wonder indeed. He will insist on offering her her freedom. I think he is wrong. I know Merya. She must know who is master, or he will have no peace. Nevertheless,' he shrugged as he took her arm to lead her towards the nursery, 'On his own head must be the consequences.'

She knew the tenderness in his nature would be roused when he saw the children, then they would sit together in the quietness that gave her her greatest happiness. Perhaps later, it would be time to tell him that in time the royal birth chair would be needed again in the royal apartments, but not yet.

We hope you have enjoyed this Large Print book. Other G.K. Hall or Chivers Press Large Print books are available at your library or directly from the publishers.

For more information about current and upcoming titles, please call or write, without obligation, to:

G.K. Hall
P.O. Box 159
Thorndike, Maine 04986
USA
Tel. (800) 223-2336

*OR*

Chivers Press Limited
Windsor Bridge Road
Bath BA2 3AX
England
Tel. (0225) 335336

All our Large Print titles are designed for easy reading, and all our books are made to last.